Nicholas E Watkins

Dealer

Dealer

Also by Nicholas E Watkins

Tanker

Bank

Oligarch

Steel

Hack

About the Author

Nicholas Watkins lives on the Coast with his wife and has four children He is a retired Accountant and has a Degree in Economics. He worked in the City of London for many years.

Dealer

Copyright © Nicholas E Watkins 2017

The right of Nicholas E Watkins to be identified as the Author of the Work has been asserted by him in accordance with the Copyright, Designs and patent Act 1988.

All rights reserved. No part of this publication my be reproduced, stored in a retrieval system, or transmitted, in any form or by any means without the prior written permission of the publisher, nor may be otherwise circulated in any form of binding or cover other than that in which it is published and without a similar condition being imposed on the subsequent purchaser.

All characters in this publication are fictional and any resemblance to real persons living or dead is purely coincidental.

Nicholas E Watkins

Chapter 1

The Dakar Rally had turned into the Argentinean Rally with a day trip to Bolivia. It had been set to run across Latin America, but Chile withdrew and Peru followed. The organisers persevered and managed to keep it on track. The stages through the Atacama Desert and the Andes disappeared in one fell swoop. The first stages would now take place on closed narrow tracks but the rally now lacked the full open stages.

Jimmy, known to all as the Driver, had financed his own team. This adventure had been in the planning stage for a long time and the dream even longer from childhood. He and his team were staying in the Poetry Building located in the Recoleta area of Buenos Aires. Although adequate, it was not ideal. It was more or less self-catering. The weather was a mix of torrential rain and searing blistering heat. The effects of El Nino seemed to become more marked with each passing year.

There was feeling of disappointment running through the team, after the first stage had been cancelled, owing to the bad weather. The Driver gathered his team together and decided on a night out to improve morale. "Let's get some good Argentinean steaks down us," he declared.

As a child, Formula One had been his initial passion. He had badgered his parents into letting him take up go-karting. His poor Father had spent nearly every weekend driving his son to meetings, spending a small fortune on machinery. He had not made the grade and rallying took its place.

Dealer

Jimmy sat in the restaurant drinking coca cola and watched his team, animated, discussing the car and all the tiny technical details. They had worked so hard to get here, he could not have wished for a more dedicated group. The smell of roasting beef filled the restaurant. There was a charcoal fire pit with the beef pinned on a frame spit in the window.

He had been good and had raced alongside Lewis Hamilton, now the World F1 champion. He had beaten him once or twice in the early years on the Karting track. The dream had slowly died. He had progressed to racing Ginettas G40s when he was fourteen. He had his moments but never had any real consistent success. He never got the wins, so the sponsorship money never came.

He remembered the day halfway through his second season when he was nearly sixteen and he had come in midway through the field at the end of the days racing. His father was driving him home. The car was on the trailer and the sun was beginning to go down, dark clouds seemed to gather in as his Father began to speak. "I am really sorry," Jimmy knew what was coming and he did not want to hear it. He felt tears welling up in his eyes as he turned his head away and stared out of the side window of the car so his Father would not see. "I just cannot afford it anymore. I've tried everywhere to obtain some sponsorship but the results are just not there. You know your Mother and I believe you can do it but…"

The sentence just hung there and that was the end of a dream for a young boy. Now the Driver was here in Argentina, ready to compete. Tomorrow would be the first real stage, approximately eleven kilometres in length. He was excited and hopeful.

The Driver had been academically gifted and put in just enough work at school to pass the GCSE's that would give him the opportunity to go to University. At eighteen he told his parents he was going to travel first. Reluctantly they agreed and again came up with the money. Looking in from the outside it was obvious that his parents indulged their only child. His Father may well have spoilt

6

him less but his Mother always took his part and indulged him. So avoiding conflict, his Father came on side and off he set on his travels with a monthly allowance.

He was nineteen and gullible. He had his twelve month round the World air ticket and his working visa for Australia and New Zealand. Young and naïve, Thailand was his first stop. A cheap hut, beaches, drink and drugs and an STD was how his first months were spent. Gradually he became a little more worldly wise and grew up a bit. He moved onto Australia and did a diving course. He did not return after his twelve month sabbatical but stayed on crewing boats and giving diving lessons.

His visa expired and now aged twenty-two arrived in San Francisco, penniless apart from the money he could wheedle from his mum. His Father had realised that any chance of Jimmy coming back and getting an education had long since gone. His Mother worshipped her son and continued to believe and support him.

He moved around the West Coast making a living as best he could. He would deal weed and take casual jobs. Never wholly criminal but on the margins he got by. He finally put his driving skills to good use. Car dealers and individuals often needed cars moved from one part of the States to another. He would drive a car from LA to New York and deliver it, then, if lucky he would pick up a commission to drive and deliver to Miami and so on back to LA. He became a preferred Driver, reliable and keeping the cars intact, he attracted work.

Hambros Benedict started to use him regularly and seemed to have cars that needed driving all over the States. He progressed from moving cars to being his driver, then into a friendship. Sitting in Benedict's apartment in Manhattan things then changed forever. The Driver sensed that Benedict had been sizing him up and scrutinizing him more and more over the previous months.

"Drink?" asked Benedict and without waiting for a reply poured a glass of red wine. The wine was expensive, so was the apartment and its furnishings. The Driver did not know what Benedict did to earn his money but he did know he earned a considerable amount of it. The apartment was in the twenty million dollar part of New York, the clothes and trappings that surrounded Benedict were in the billionaire spectrum of wealth.

"You have been working for me for a while now." The Driver said nothing. "I like you." The Driver feared that an awkward gay moment was on the way, but not so.

"I am getting on and want to have time, well in a cliché, want to have some time before I die to enjoy the fortunes of my labours." The Driver was confused but nodded his understanding. He knew that Benedict's wife and young daughter had died many years ago in a tragic car crash. He also knew that he had recently taken to a young mistress. A gold digger, but he could afford it and it made him happy, it certainly was none of the Driver's business.

"I have been looking to ease out of the business for a while now but in my line of work that is easier said than done." The Driver had no idea what Benedict's line of business was and wondered if he should ask or just wait for the conversation to develop. He waited.

"Do you know what I do?" before the Driver could reply. "Arms" said Benedict

"I don't understand?"

"I source weapons and broker a deal between buyers and sellers. There is always conflict in the World and Governments and individuals need the right tools to deal with problems. In this case it is the right gun, missile, bomb or tank. I supply the tools and make a commission. No different to selling realty or insurance. You just need the right contacts and the skills to negotiate, plus a willingness to do a lot of travel."

There was a silence as he allowed the Driver to absorb what had been said. He began to speak but Benedict held up his hand to silence him. "I am getting old and this is a young man's game. The travel no longer appeals and the negotiating is a stress I can do without. Now you are bright and young."

Over the next six years the Driver took on more and more and Benedict got his retirement. The Driver was now working on his own and working for himself. He was an international arms dealer but Benedict had left him in the small league. The deals could involve countless million to finance. True, the Driver had millions but to get into the big time he needed more. The next deal would change all that, but in the meantime there was racing to be done.

The beef was the best and he and the crew relaxed laughed and ate their fill. The rain briefly stopped as they made their way back to their apartments. The Driver and Enrich Sloganeer sat down over the timing sheets and route map in the apartment they shared. The next day was a prologue to the rally proper. It was eleven kilometres and Sloganeer was one of the best navigators to be had. He had never done the Dakar but had co-driven with the best in the World and won rally championships. The Driver was determined to make this his race. He had spent as much on his car and team as the works teams. They drove the stage in their minds one more time before heading for the bedroom and sleep.

The Driver sped away from the start, Sloganeer calling the track, "Left, right, right, break, power, power." The information came loud and clear, thick and fast through the headset. The adrenaline coursed through their veins as they bounced, skidded and jumped their way through the stage. The Driver was elated. He lived for this. The spectators crowded the track, excited and eager to glimpse the speeding cars at the limits of man and machine.

Then it stopped, as if in slow motion the car slid. The Drive tried to correct, over corrected then lost control. The car rolled over and over. The spectators tried to scatter and still the car rolled, then, silence and black, ten injured, two spectators and Sloganeer dead, the stage cancelled. The dream was over.

Chapter 2

New York was as cold as Buenos Aires had been wet. The snow had been pushed from the roads but Manhattan was still struggling after the cold snap. The three Russians in the stretched limo had been used to the cold in Moscow, but now they were more accustomed to the warmth and sunshine of the Cote Azure or the tropical islands of the Caribbean. With the wind chill it was twenty below on the sidewalks.

"Don't you miss Russia when you see this weather?" asked Vasiliev Nikhil. He was a man in his late fifties, almost bald with a long straight nose, which had been broken on various occasions in the past. The elegance of his attire could not mask the fact that he was a man hard in nature and unforgiving in attitude. In fact his two companions, Sokolov Yerik and Volkov Lesta, shared the hard edge. They were of a similar age and had met at the Andropov KGB spy school in Russia. They had worked in the intelligence services for most of their careers until their fortunes changed and Russia became a free for all, almost the Wild West, when Boris Yeltsin gave up the Presidency.

"Do I fuck," said Lesta. They were driving past Central Park and the "Trump Ice Rink" was up and running. "See it is like Gorky Park," he pointed through the window.

"Good idea, we should put our names up and charge for skating," said Yerik.

"We should walk down Seventh," said Lesta, "they are selling things cheaply."

"You seem to forget we are now honest hard working businessmen and rich. We only have the best. If it is on sale then it means people did not want it so they sell cheaply. If other people did not want it then it is not good enough for us," said Yerik.

"You are just getting to be a fat and lazy bastard," said Nikhil.

"I am not a bastard," They all laughed, he could not argue the fat or lazy.

The limo continued down town to the New York Stock exchange and Wall Street. It stopped, the Driver rolled back the divide." It is down there, I cannot make a turn here." He started to get out of the car to open the doors as he spoke.

"It is OK, my friend is not yet so fat and lazy he cannot open his car door." The Driver smiled and thought to himself that they were definitely a pair of bastards even if they were not fat, but said nothing as they exited.

Mel Levy had them shown into his office. He was nervous. He needed these people to back him. After the collapse in the banking system, owing to the credit crunch, he had found himself exposed and overstretched. With no access to borrowing he had gone from the darling hedge fund manger of Wall Street to one of its biggest fraudsters. He was out of jail now, had his freedom and little else but his brain. These men needed him to solve their problem. He knew it would all depend on personality. It always did.

"Good morning, I am Mel Levy."

"We know who you are but do you know who we are?" said Nikhil.

Levy was unsure how to respond. He certainly knew who they were. They were, what the World now called, Russian oligarchs. They were people who had seized, their opportunity, when Russia was in a state of flux, to grab large chunks, of the old industries, from the State for themselves. They were the modern day equivalent of the old Wild West "carpet baggers." His dilemma was, should he just openly say they were a bunch of crooks or should he play the respected business men game? He thought and replied trusting his instinct,

"You are, I fear, the same as me, crooks."

There was silence. Levy felt the tension. "Yerik broke the silence. " My day is getting better I have been promoted from a fat, lazy bastard to crook." The atmosphere eased as they all laughed.

"To business?" asked Levy. They nodded and he began to explain his strategy for extracting their and their colleague's wealth. Billions of dollars and shielding it from US lead sanctions against Russia, that were put in place after the annexation of the Crimean peninsular from the Ukraine. They all knew that the Americans were determined to hit the likes of Yerik, Nikhil and Lesta in the pocket, where it would really hurt and exert pressure for policy change.

"Iceland has a problem and we have a solution," began Levy. "They have depositor's money locked up in their banks and cannot return it without collapsing their banks and their economy. We have the solution."

The scheme was complex and he took his time explaining. They listened for over an hour and questions were raised. Yerik finally spoke to summarise. "So we will be the owners of the Baltic Bank and we will allow any and all depositors, with the consent of the Icelandic regulators, to transfer their fund from the existing banks into our Bank?"

"It comes at a cost of twenty percent to the depositors. For example they have one hundred dollars in the Icelandic bank, when the transfer they have eighty hundred dollars in the Baltic Bank," said Levy.

We wash our and our partner's dirty money through a special purpose Bank in Vanuatu, where there are no real checks, to give them their money anywhere in the world. Ostensibly, it is their deposits we are refunding but is in fact our money now nice and clean, laundered as the say?" continued Yerik.

"The Icelandic government will need to levy between ten and fifteen per cent on deposits held there. It is the same savings grab used in Cyprus if they are to keep afloat. We have factored in twenty so we should even make a profit," said Levy.

"Why would the Icelandic regulators go for it that is what I don't understand?" said Lesta.

"They are not going for anything. They are just allowing money to move internally and we will ensure there is sufficient liquidity to allow their banks can keep trading. They need to re-establish credibility with the depositors. This does it for them. They can do detailed checks on the source of funds and technically have clean money in their system, from the Baltic Banks holding company, in Vanuatu. Everybody ticks the right boxes and they move on, until the next banking scandal hits the markets at least."

"Let's do it."

"I must highlight the only weakness to you. You have to sign the papers I am about to give you in your own names and have them notarised. These signatures will link you to the money you have, shall we say, invested overseas. They need to be shown to the regulators in Iceland. But beyond that they will be kept secure, away from prying eyes," said Levy.

"Do we have a choice?" said Lesta.

"No"

They signed and handed the papers back to Levy. "Congratulations Gentlemen, you are now bankers," he said.

Chapter 3

Adnan and Nizar waited on the Turkish Syrian border for the convoy of trucks to arrive. Nizar had just found himself in charge of the ISIS led forces in the North, following a successful US drone attack on the previous incumbent.

"When are they due?" he asked.

"It could be an hour, it could be a few days. It is the nature of the process. It is not like popping to the local shops," replied Adnan.

The rebellion in Syria started in 2011 following the success of the so-called Arab spring that saw regime changes in Libya and Egypt. ISIS, by the middle of 2014 had become the main anti-government force. By 2015 Qatar, Saudi Arabia and Turkey were openly backing the various groups making up, what they called, the Army of Conquest. ISIS was now in control of a third of Syrian territory and most of its oil and gas production.

Nizar sat in the truck cab with Adnan and waited. In the back of the flat bed sat six further armed ISIS fighters. The food and basic supplies were running well but he decided that he should check out the situation and get to know for himself the nuts and bolts of the supply process. The supply lines were virtually immune from air attack running through Turkey, which being part of NATO could not be attacked by the opposition forces. The Turks defended their air space vigorously and had even shot down a Russian fighter that had encroached. The trade routes also extended outwards southwest where friends in West Jordan and Saudi Arabia aided them and extended the logistics network that covered Eastern Europe and Africa.

Nizar was, however, struggling with the supply of arms. In 2011, weapons left over in from NATO's intervention in Libya were sent to Turkey and then ended up in Syria. The CIA had virtually set up an arms depot in the annex to the US Consulate in Benghazi to supply arms to Syrian Rebels, a lot of these weapons ended up with ISIS. Recently it had become increasingly difficult to keep his army fully equipped. Whilst they had recycled mortars, light arms which had been taken from opposing forces, ammunition, to feed the guns was a constant headache.

So far the Russian air strikes had been firmly targeted to help the President, Bashar al-Assad, to overcome the immediate threat to his regime and had not had a much impact on ISIS activity, but Nizar knew that it was only a matter of time until international pressure changed all that. He wanted to be ready and he knew that he needed to re-equip.

Adnan interrupted his thoughts. "They come."

Nizar looked up to see the convoy arrive. Thirty articulated trucks just rolled over the border unhindered. Turkey's ambiguous political stance and the greed of the highest officials to the lowest border guards made it all so easy.

Adnan jumped out of the Toyota pick-up and Nizar followed. The Drivers of the trucks alighted and made their way to a coach that would take them back home to Turkey. The opposite process was taking place on this side of the border. The ISIS Drivers disembarked from the coach, parked two hundred metres from the Toyota and made their way to the now vacant cabs of the articulated trucks. They would take over the driving for the Syrian leg of the journey.

Adnan approached the two men that had accompanied the convoy in the air conditioned Mercedes. Nizar followed and observed. The process was simple. A tablet was produced and the internet connection made. The transfer of funds over, the parties would return to their vehicles and set off.

"That is all there is to it," said Adnan as they drove back into Syria.

"We have beans and rice but we need guns and ammunition. That is our problem. It is getting harder to source the weapons we need to keep the momentum going."

"We are doing our best but the international pressure is building. Even the British are being put under pressure over their arms supplies to the Saudis. The old sources like Croatia are just simply running out of armaments to sell. It is hard."

"There are other sources," said Nizar.

"There are and there are other conflicts that the arms dealers can make their profits from that they do not run up against the CIA. The US has more sympathy for these other causes and do not conflict with American interests. Given the choice of making an easy buck in Latin America or Africa, why would you put yourself in the CIA firing line?"

"I have had all the commanders' reports assed and given to me. It is clear we need re-supplying on a vast scale. It cannot go on as it is. The Russians will turn their forces on us eventually. Sooner or later they will work with the US. They need to. At the moment their interest lies historically with supporting Assad ,so they are attacking the rebels forces that are closest to overthrowing him, but that will change. They need to improve relations with the West and they will turn on us in their own self interest. We need to be ready."

"There is a man. They call him The Driver. He worked for a major player who has left the arms dealing business."

"Can he get what we want?"

There was a moments silence as they bounced along the road at the rear of the long convoy. Adnan considered what he knew of this man. The truth was he knew very little. As head of procurement for ISIS in Syria he knew how vulnerable they could be to CIA stings. Going to a new source was risky. If this Driver was a CIA front man then they could lose money and personnel and at the same time hand a lot of valuable information to the opposition. He knew Nizar was under a lot of pressure to take firm control of the situation. The constant targeted attack on the leading figures by drones and strikes were having the desired effect on the command on the ground. The truth has always been the same, an army is only as good as its supply lines and those supply lines were beginning to creak.

"We have no choice. We need to make contact. In fact, I need to make contact. There is too much at stake and too much money involved, just to leave the negotiations to an intermediary," replied Adnan.

He knew Adnan was right, but he could not afford to lose him to a CIA sting. "Must you negotiate personally?"

"I will contact the Driver." There was no more to be said as they drove deeper into ISIS held territory.

Chapter 4

Elaine Wilkins had settled quite comfortably into her role as head of MI5, which is more than could be said for the latest pair of shoes she was wearing. She was sat in the River Room in the Savoy Hotel with her deputy Jeff Stiles. They had managed to get a window seat overlooking the Thames. The air was damp and there was a slight mist forming in the fine drizzle that fell on London.

"How did you manage to get a table at such short notice?" asked Jeff.

"I didn't. I am supposed to be having lunch with the Home Secretary, his office booked it. He cancelled, so I thought, what the hell, let's treat ourselves anyway."

"Why would that mean bugger be buying you lunch?"

"What, you don't think I warrant a free scoff on MP's expenses?" She smiled. "You're right, though there is no such thing as a free lunch. I am guessing it is to do with this Select Committee looking into arms sales to the Saudis."

"He was business trade and what not minister, before he got the Home Secretary job wasn't he? When is he due to appear?"

"Some time next week. It is a tricky one really. The Saudis are big spenders and the arms manufacturers need the business," said Elaine.

"Only problem is that the Saudis seem to be funding and supplying arms to Syria and the Yemen, supporting Al-Qaeda and ISIS. We just keep granting "End User Certificates" knowing that the arms are being used to kill women, children and the civilian population all over the Middle East." Manufacturers, or anyone exporting arms, are subject to the Export Control Organisation rules that require them to provide information as to the final destinations of the weapons and an assessment of risk of the arms falling into the wrong hands at the licensing stage.

"I think the inquiry has pretty much noticed that no export licenses have ever been turned down."

"Just goes to show what good guys the arms dealers' are." said Jeff.

"Or just how skewed the system is in favour of the exporters."

"What's that got to do with us?" he said.

The waiter interrupted their conversation with Elaine's Caesar salad. They sat in silence as the waiter went through his bit of theatre preparing the salad at the table. Jeff had to admit, watching the waiter going through the ritual of making the dressing and delicately arranging the leaves on the plate did somehow make you feel as if your money had been well spent on, essentially, a bit of lettuce, dressing and a few bits of fried bread. Jeff had avoided the healthy eating option and had gone for lamb, cooked in various ways and vegetables.

"Yours looks nice," said Stiles with little sincerity.

"It's an age thing, you'll get old one day and your belly will start to overtake your chest."

"Getting back to the dear old Minister, what does he want from you?"

"Well, you know in the Falklands war, some of the weapons we sold abroad were used against us in the conflict? He is trying to head off the Committee at the pass and avoid, at least, the accusation that exported arms have ended up in the hands of

Jihadis who are committing acts of terrorism in Europe or here."

"And are they?"

"You should know," she said

"Well they are of course, but I meant what is the position we are adopting?"

"Tricky isn't it? It is a bit of the Donald Rumsfeld logic, how did it go?

Jeff took out his mobile phone and read" There are known knowns. These are things we know that we know. There are known unknowns. That is to say, there are things that we know we don't know. But, there are also unknown unknowns. There are things we don't know we don't know." He laughed.

"Exactly our position," said Elaine,

"In other words you were going to give him a, we suspect and know but cannot prove it, answer."

"Well it does not pay to hang the Hone Secretary out to dry. It cuts both ways, we will fuck up at some stage and we need friends at Westminster."

"Doesn't politics just give you a warm glow of satisfaction? Anyway enough of that, how's the family?"

"My husband's no better."

"I am sorry"

"Don't be. I have mentally prepared myself for the inevitable. My son is doing well and prospering in business land making money. Something we won't do in this job. How is yours?"

"They are well thank you." He replied as the waiter cleared the plates. "There is one small point on security that might be pertinent to your brief to the Minister. I am getting reports that ISIS or Al Qaeda fighters in Syria are in the market for a big buy of arms. We and the US are supplying the rebels, who are not allied to ISIS, with hardware, but have put pressure on them to source their own."

"What was the source?"

"GCHQ have picked up traffic on the web showing they are looking for brokers and dealers in the UK. Someone is operating here but seems to keep just off the radar." GCHQ is the Government's eyes and ears and is situated just outside of Cheltenham, constantly monitoring all forms of communication. It is responsible to the Secretary of State for the British and Commonwealth and is not part of the Foreign Office as such.

"More of an MI6 problem really," said Elaine.

""True, but I thought I would liaise with Special Branch and just do a bit of digging. It does no harm to know who is operating on our patch and might just lead us to some links to potential terrorists based here."

"We have scarce resources and following arms deals for export does not seem a good use of what we have. Does it?"

"You know me, I am nosey and like to keep my ear to the ground."

"On this occasion you'll just have to curb your natural curiosity. Let's order a taxi, I think I may have problems making the entrance lobby in these shoes."

Chapter 5

The bus terminal in Istanbul was packed. The three girls were struggling to force their way through the unruly crowd that pushed and shoved their way onto the departing coaches. The crowd did not form orderly queues to board but mobbed each bus. It was a totally alien environment to their daily lives in Walsall, near Birmingham in England. They had set out in the early hours of the previous day from their home town. The Big Red Bus had delivered them at Victoria in London. They had taken the Gatwick express to the Airport and spent an uncomfortable night sleeping there, before catching the early morning flight to Turkey.

None of the girls had been abroad before, apart from a school trip to France. Mariam and Haniya were fifteen and in the same class at their local faith school. Aleena was Mariam's younger sister by a year. Mariam had been the prime mover behind this trip. Eighteen months ago she had begun exploring her sense of self and her faith. In a very short time she found herself talking to a young woman, called Fatin, on an Islamic site. Over a period of months their friendship grew and Fatin told Mariam the joy of living as a true Muslim. She related to her how she had found happiness and contentment in her marriage to true Muslim man. She also described how handsome and brave he was. How he fought for his beliefs, a true hero.

As time progressed, their conversation, like their friendship became more intimate. Fatin would send her tracks, commentaries on the Qur'an, showing the true meaning of the Holy Book. How life could be idyllic if she lived life as the Prophet described it. Soon, Mariam began to see how the West was corrupting the true way of life and how they were waging war against Islam.

She began talking to her sister Aleena and her best friend Haniya. At first it was like having a secret that they shared, almost an adventure game. Soon they were all in regular contact with Fatin and her words and vision of Islam became more and more beguiling to the girls.

A sexual tension grew in the girls, fed by Fatin with her visions of strong handsome warriors fighting for their God, These young men became heroes to the girls. The picture was painted of them fighting against the evil forces of the West, defending the poor and the oppressed and forging a path of freedom for their downtrodden brothers and sisters. It was a romantic picture of the life and aims of the Jihadis in Syria.

Gradually, Fatin turned the conversation to the stoicism and lonely devoted life of these heroes. She relayed how she was a true obedient wife to one such fighter. She lived in paradise as a true Muslim without the defilement and the corruption that was imposed by the West. She described her life of pure bliss living as a devoted and obedient wife to a great fighter.

The seduction was complete, the instructions as to how to save money, how to use their parent's credit card to buy plane tickets and what to pack for the trip came in the emails. The pressure built and the young girls, fully immersed in the fantasy, set off to Syria. They were eager, excited in the anticipation of meeting their brave, handsome new husbands.

The coach trip across from Istanbul to the Syrian border was, in truth, the worst thing the three had experienced in their lives. Life in their comfortable homes in England had not prepared them for the rigours of Turkish travel. They had never encountered the Arab style toilet with two raised foot shaped pads to stand on and a hole to defecate in. Squatting and relieving themselves was almost impossible for them, not having the necessary flexibility in their ankle joints, having been used to sitting on a western style toilet all their lives. The bucket and sponge had further added to their discomfort. The food was alien and all three had stomach bugs, making their trips to the alien toilets more frequent.

They stepped from the bus dehydrated with badly upset stomachs, exhausted and weak. The crossing was manned and documents were being inspected. They looked at each other and realised they stood out from the crowd, the guards were already glancing suspiciously in their direction long before it was their turn to present their papers.

Unknown to the three back in the UK, their parents had already raised the alarm. The police had already cracked their emails and knew they were headed for Turkey. The press had the story and their whole lives were being microscopically examined. They did not know it, but they were on the run. They were now part of a game, political and ideological they had no real understanding of.

In an instant they were seized by the Turkish border guards and led away to a small locked room where they were left while phone calls were made. Aleena began to sob as the whole experience translated from a romantic fantasy into the reality of sitting tired, hungry and unwell in a stifling small room.

Adnan, the second in command to the new ISIS leader Nizar, was the first to get a call. He was waiting across the border for their arrival. The guards were in regular contact with the fighters in Syria. Not friends, but grateful of the income the smuggling activities brought the them

The next recipient of a call was Mehmet, the deputy head of Turkish security. Mehmet had been educated in the West and with his connections to the ruling elites he had risen rapidly in his post. He was a feared man. To cross him was a very bad thing to do. His sophisticated western veneer when scratched revealed a totally ruthless man who was totally self serving. He would do what it takes to serve himself and his country. He would murder, torture, prostitute women and children. He was a man with no moral compass and used his position to satisfy his desires without concern for the victims. Highly intelligent, he was a sociopath and never hesitated in following his baser instincts with no remorse. He was a very dangerous individual who served his masters exceedingly well.

The pressure was on Turkey to find and return the girls to the UK and Mehmet knew this. On the other hand, there were other considerations to be taken into account, not least the large bribe he had just been offered by Adnan to let the girls cross into Syria. There was a working relationship and common interest as well as conflict between Turkey and the various groups that operated in Syria. The strange situation had developed into such a state of confusion that one ISIS faction could be carrying out suicide bombings in Turkey while the Turks would be lending air, or even ground support to another ISIS faction fighting the Kurds. The, your enemy is my enemy therefore you are my friend, logic played out in the region daily.

"Adnan it's Mehmet" he called the Jihadi. "I am not sure about this one. There is a lot of flack. It might well just be easier to send the three slags back home?"

"We have worked hard on this. The fact that it is high profile is what we wanted. It draws attention to the Arab cause. It inspires other Muslims to join us. It attacks them in the own homes, the brothers, sisters and children are all potential fighters for God," said Adnan.

"Yeah I know all that but you will forgive me if I don't share your vision of paradise and deal with the reality of Turkish interests at home and abroad."

"Three thousand dollars"

"Six"

"Five," said Adnan.

Mehmet paused, "I'll see what I can do."

A half an hour later the border post received a phone call."

"Go," said the guard and pushed the girls across the border on foot, the bus having left hours before.

They were near collapse when Adnan spotted them. He waived to the waiting car from the truck where he had been seated observing. Two young men approached the girls and led them to the vehicle and drove off. Adnan drove in the opposite direction into Turkey, he had an arms shipment to sort and these girls had already cost him too much time and effort.

Chapter 6

Volkov Lesta sat back in his chair at the Mikhailovsky Theatre in St Petersburg. Tonights performance was Tosca and he was not looking forward to it. He considered himself more of a practical person than a lover of the arts. The prospect of sitting through a couple of hours of some women wailing about her lover then flinging herself off the battlements when he gets himself hung did not appeal at all. Dmytro Dovzhenko did however find it appealing and had specifically requested his usual visit to the theatre when meeting up with Lesta.

Lesta had known Dovzhenko since before the break up of the Soviet Union and they had owned a little black market business together, when times had been hard. Lesta's KGB connection had allowed Dovzhenko to carry on doing his dodgy business dealings without fear of police intervention. It had been beneficial to both of them in the lean times.

As Dovzhenko sat back to enjoy the opera, Lesta allowed his mind to drift onto to the matter in hand. He knew that Dovzhenko had gotten himself into a tight spot. The Ukraine had, over the past few years, been engaged in a civil war with large parts of the population with ethnic ties to Russia wanting closer integration with the Motherland and the remainder wanting to move towards the West. Russia was supporting the one and the West financing the other. As part of the conflict, Russia had seized back the Crimean Peninsula and the West, and in Particular the United States, had imposed sanctions, the very sanctions that he, Yerik and Nikhil were getting round with their joint enterprise in the Baltic bank. Dovzhenko did not have the problem of laundering his money. In fact his problem was the opposite in that he had no money.

Dovzhenko was Ukrainian and after the break up had found himself sitting on the other side of the border. There were opportunities to be had, one of the most profitable was the military hardware left over in the former Soviet states. The Soviet Union had abandoned literally tons of arms when the split had come and the so called Cold War finished. Dovzhenko with his connections to Lesta and with some funding had started up in the arms business. He picked up arms cheaply, or just helped himself in some cases, where the former storage facilities had just been left unguarded in the chaos immediately following the Russians departure from their former territories.

The trade had been good and the profits vast. He and Lesta had become immensely wealthy. Lesta had diversified into the opportunities that appeared in Russia itself and increased his fortune in the timber industry. Dovzhenko had stuck with what he knew, arms dealing. He had seen the Russian Ukrainian conflict as a massive opportunity and went on an arms buying spree in anticipation. It did not pan out as he expected and now he had vast stockpiles and no way of shifting them.

Lesta knew that his old friend would be looking to borrow from him, or more precisely the Baltic Bank. Nikhil, Yerik and he had been busy with their new bank. They were now making fortunes laundering money for Oligarchs and Dictators across the Globe and making loans at high rates of interest to fund all kinds of illicit activity, from drug dealing and people trafficking to arms dealing.

The chairs at the Mikhailovsky Theatre, which admittedly were very attractive, were not however conducive to comfort and Lesta was feeling his bum going numb. The chairs were more like carvers than theatre seats and he felt that this was definitely a case of style over substance. They had the interval and had a few shots of vodka. Now, he wanted a pee and to stretch his legs. He focused back on the action. Tosca had just visited her lover in the slammer and he was about to get the chop. Not long now, he thought, a bit more caterwauling and she would sling herself off the walls. It was a relief when they stood up to applaud and the circulation returned to his neither regions.

Back in the Imperial Suite at the Hermitage Museum Hotel the vodka was opened and the food was on the table. Lesta and Dovzhenko settled down to eat supper. The eating phase was short but the vodka stage continued as they settled in round the coffee table.

"Where are we are at?" said Lesta.

"Volkov, we have known each other for many years."

"I know that Dmytro, but we both know that this is not just a social call."

Lesta continued. "No it isn't but I need help. So who else should I come to? I am sure you know I have too much stock and not enough buyers. It is bleeding me dry, storage costs, security, warehousing, light and heat. Money and more money."

"You need a good conflict, my friend."

"I thought I had one in my home country, but you Russians and the Americans are supplying both sides direct for free and have cut out the middleman."

"Annoying of them and both, such good capitalists, who would have thought it?" joked Lesta.

Dovzhenko allowed himself a smile and took another swig of vodka before continuing," Five million."

Lesta sat and studied his old friend. It was a small amount in terms of the arms trade. He knew that Dovzhenko had nearly three hundred million dollars worth of weaponry ready to be shipped. He also knew that if the loan went into default that he couldn't just turn up with a repossession order and sell the guns off at the local auction. He sat quietly and sipped his vodka.

"Where and when will you be able to repay? Do you have a buyer?"

It was clear from the expression on Dovzhenko's face that he did not. He shrugged his shoulders and sat quietly. It was clear to Lesta that this was a man out of options.

"You know that I would be mad to lend you this money. Tell me how much are you in for?" Lesta knew the answer already but wanted to know that Dovzhenko would tell him the truth.

"Ninety five million and if you advance the five then a round hundred million"

He was being truthful. The silence hung between them. It was not a negotiating ploy on Lesta's part. He was genuinely unsure if he wanted to be involved, after all he was making big bucks letting the Chinese chop down tress and hauling them off without lifting a finger and his share of the money laundering, using the dodgy Baltic Bank and its subsidiaries, was bringing in goodly amount. Greed got the better of him, unsurprisingly.

"I will give you one hundred and ten million for the lot."

Dovzhenko's jaw nearly hit the floor as the offer sank in. He went through a range of emotions from shock to anger ending with a nervous laugh. "You are joking of course? They are worth five times that."

"Only if you can find a buyer and only if you can find a buyer fast enough. Do you have a buyer?"

He knew he didn't have a buyer and if he did not have the five million within a few days, he knew it would be in no position to find one as the people in the arms trade were not the sort of people to let you run up debts. Either you paid up or you became a paid up member of the graveyard club. "One hundred and fifty"

Lesta knew he had him. "One hundred million, my next offer will be lower"

"I'll take the one hundred and ten"

Lesta let his friend sweat. "OK, one hundred and ten million. Now let's drink to it."

They did drink to it and they carried on drinking vodka throughout the night. They passed out on the chairs and woke with raging thirsts and even more raging headaches. It was like being young again, only the hangovers were worse and Lesta felt like his liver wanted to leave his body and go on holiday. Finally, they sobered up enough to walk and continue the rest of their day.

Dovzhenko stood in the doorway and asked the question. "Do you have a buyer?"

"I think I may well do," smiled Lesta.

"You fucking smug bastard, you never change," was Dovzhenko's parting comment as he closed the door behind him.

Chapter 7

It was the Sunday morning of the race and the despite the rain the streets of Monaco were filled with race goers. It was the day of the Grand Prix. The crowds moved around the town, passing the stalls that lined the side roads and the approach to the seating erected around the track.

The Jimmy, the Driver could not miss such an event and his mentor, and former boss Hambros Benedict, had invited him. Having retired from the arms broking business, he had bought a multi million Euro apartment over looking the course. From his balcony he had the perfect view of the circuit, where the formula one cars powered up the hill, before descending the gradient to the harbour.

The Driver had arrived that morning via helicopter from Nice Airport. He was greeted warmly by Benedict as he entered the apartment. Though slightly garish, the furnishings were a mix a contemporary with what the Driver assumed to be very expensive antique statement pieces.

"The apartment is amazing," he said to Benedict.

"My wife, she has the eye and designed the whole place herself."

"How is ..?"

"Mimi," he finished the sentence, "she is fine and lively as ever."

There was a slight awkward pause and the Driver moved towards the balcony. Benedict pressed a button on the remote he had picked up from the coffee table and the blinds slowly ascended, allowing the grey morning light to filter into the room. The Driver slide the windows open and stepped out onto the large terrace. Another button was pressed on the remote and the sun canopy unfurled itself and acted as an umbrella. The rain had just increased in intensity and the view from the terrace towards the harbour was obscured by the haze.

"Not the best day for a Grand Prix and not the easiest circuit in the wet," he observed.

"Hamilton needs the win and he is good in the rain. I think he has the edge over Roseburg in these conditions but they are both so good it will be close," said Benedict. They walked back inside and moved to the dining room. A young man appeared and poured the coffee. The table was laid with cereal, fruit and croissants. They sat. "Would you prefer a cooked breakfast?"

"No I am fine. I ate on the plane, sort of."

"It is nice to see you again," said Benedict warmly. They had grown close over the years in the high pressure environment of the arms trade. A kind of affection had grown between them over that time, a mixture of trust and paternal feelings on Benedict's part. With the loss of his wife and daughter some of that affection had been transferred to the Driver.

There was a noise from another part of the apartment and the door opened. Mimi stepped into the dining room. "Hi, nice to see you again," she said to the Driver as she bent over to kiss Benedict.

She was wearing a completely see through wrap made of the most diaphanous, translucent fabric the Driver had ever seen. He could not fail to be impressed with her body. She was Pilipino in origin and her beauty was undeniable, she made sure she displayed as much of it as she could for men to admire. As she leaned forward to kiss her husband her breasts hung away from her body and the Driver could see the dark raised nipples revealed as the wrap gaped.

The young man entered and poured coffee. The wrap was beginning to unwrap and one of her breasts was fully exposed. She made no attempt to cover it as the young mans eyes openly lingered on her. The Driver watched Benedict and saw that he was watching the reaction from the waiter. He clearly enjoyed his wife's exhibitionism.

"I am excited about the party tonight," she said to her husband, "it has been a while since I have had some real fun." Turning to the Driver she asked. "Will you be here?"

"Of course he will. He is here for the weekend."

She turned and looked again at the Driver. It was a provocative look. She continued to question her husband. "Who is coming?"

"Lots of old friends, Jill and Marie, with their husbands of course and lots of young men, some you haven't met," he said.

"Lots?"

"Lots," he confirmed. "I need to have a quite word with our friend here in private, so you organize lunch with Chef while we talk a little business."

The Driver was puzzled by the conversation Benedict had with Mimi. "Are you married?" he asked as they moved into the office.

"Spur of the moment thing. I am getting old and so, why not, live out a few fantasies," he smiled.

"Congratulations"

"Thank you. Now, are you still in the business?"

"You would be forgiven in thinking I had retired but I am still working. It is just that the traditional markets are not there. Latin America has quietened down and the Chinese are catering to Africa," said the Driver.

"There is no shortage of demand in the Middle East, Iraq and Syria."

"It was never our area and I just don't have the contacts."

"Well someone is looking to make contact and has been asking about you. An Arab chap called Adnan. Heard of him?"

"Not a dicky, who is he?"

"To be honest I haven't that much interest these days but he is with one of the factions fighting against Al-Assad in Syria. When I say ISIS it could be Al Qaeda, but now of course they claim to be unconnected and merely freedom fighters hoping to get support from the Americans. The US isn't having any of it and won't arm them. So they are out in the market place looking to acquire quite a lot of hardware."

"Not the best idea to go head to head with the Americans though."

"That is true of course, but it is also true that if you do and succeed than there is big money to be had."

"How large?" Since his ill fated expedition to Argentina and the Dakar rally the Driver had been mostly inactive. The loss of his co-Driver and the deaths of the spectators had left him with a decline in confidence. He sold weapons, but in truth had never been close to their actual use. It was a business transaction and remote. The Driver had learnt one thing from the experience and that was that he was a coward. Like all cowards he knew that he would do anything if push came to shove to save his own neck.

"Close to three million dollars worth of ammo, ground to air, rifles, RPGs and machine guns. All small stuff, but a lot of it."

"Shame they don't want a tank or two, less to move about and much higher value."

"They have no air cover, anything big would be obliterated by Assad, the Yanks and its allies, or even the Russians if they deicide to change policy and hit ISIS as well as the direct opposition to the President."

"How do I meet him, this Adnan?"

"He will be at the party tonight."

The rain cleared up just after the start of the race, they had an amazing view, drinking champagne and sitting on the terrace. Their nostrils were filed with the smell of high octane fuel and their ears deafened by the raw power of the Formula One car engines. The race had all the thrills that Monaco can bring to the event. Verstappen crashing at the start, safety cars, rain and virtual safety cars were all part of the spectacle that day. Hamilton won the race and the Driver could only think back to his go-karting days and dream of what might have been.

Chapter 8

The three girls Mariam, her younger sister Aleena and Haniya had been travelling for days. It was hard for them to reconcile the reality of the situation in Syria, with the romantic picture they had been encouraged to form in their minds by the woman they knew as Fatin. They were in the back of a dusty bouncing truck. Their western clothes had been taken and swapped for traditional dress. Only their eyes were visible as the truck drove past bombed, collapsed buildings and craters in the road. They were very young and very afraid.

"When do we meet Fatin?" Mariam had asked ask when they boarded the truck, just after they had crossed the border from Turkey.

The men had just laughed and responded vaguely that it would be soon. The subject was ignored from there on in as were most of the questions posed by the three girls. Mariam clung to the vision she had created in Walsall, whereas her sister and Haniya were experiencing severe doubts as to their fate. The reality was a far cry from the picture Mariam had painted.

Haniya's period had started a day ago. She had gone to her backpack to recover the tampons she needed. It was at that point that the situation they had put themselves in was rammed home. The young man who had done most of the driving had observed her, He was dressed in the obligatory battle fatigues and was never far from his automatic rifle. The first thing the girls had become aware of was how badly their two hosts stank. They made no attempt at personal hygiene and seemed immune to the stink of their mutual body odour. The Driver was the worst by far. Small in stature with bandy legs, he was far removed from the Jihadi heroes the girls had seen on the internet and he stank.

"What the fuck are you doing?" he shouted as he got to his feet and walked towards Haniya.

She showed him the box of tampons. "It is my time of the month."

He snatched them from her hand and threw them into the ditch that ran along side the road. "Stinking western whore," he ranted.

The other man stepped forward and placed a restraining hand on the Driver's shoulder. "Forgive my friend he comes from a very strict background where the girls are kept intact. Their grandmothers usually attend to these things when they are eight or nine," he led his friend away.

Haniya was at first puzzled and shocked. "What did he mean?" she asked Mariam.

There was a look of fear and horror on her friends face. "Circumcision"

The penny dropped and Haniya felt panic rise. Aleena was confused and frightened at her sister and her friends obvious upset. "I don't understand?"

They tried to explain that it was common in some Muslim countries, like Egypt, for the grandmother to cut the clitoris from the young girls and remove the labia and stitch the opening virtually shut leaving a small hole for urination and menstruation. Aleena felt sick and began to tremble.

"The hole they leave is too small to insert a tampon and even touching down there would be seen as wanton."

They got back on the truck severally shaken by the realisation as to how fundamental some of the fighters were in their beliefs. All

Haniya could do was tear up a blouse, roll it into a pad and stuff it into her knickers.

They spent another uncomfortable night sleeping by the truck. They all had terrible diarrhoea from the food and the lack of hygiene by the time they reached camp. Weak and shaky, they were led from the truck to be surrounded by a group of unkempt men, who shouted as they were stood in the centre of the circle that formed around them.

Frightened and confused only Mariam found her voice, "Where is Fatin?"

She was greeted with a roar of laughter from the group. A man in his late forties, balding and filthy stepped forward. "I am Fatin." His statement was greeted by even louder laughter from the assembled.

Aleena clung to her sister, tears in her eyes. "Why are you saying that?"

"You cannot be that stupid?" mocked the man. "Fatin is a fantasy on the web, no more and no less." The realisation that they were nothing to these men finally sank in. They were there to satisfy them and act as propaganda.

An elderly overweight woman dressed in a black Abaya that stretched from her head to the ground emerged from a tent and made her way over to the new arrivals. She beckoned the girls to come into the tent. They obeyed, glad to be away from the leering group.

The tent smelt of urine and cooking fat, it took some while for their eyes to adjust to the dim interior. Three further women came into focus as their eyes adjusted. "Take off your undergarments."

The girls hesitated and looked at one another. Aleena was siezed by the woman and pulled towards a filthy mattress in one corner. "Now," said the woman aggressively. Aleena reluctantly removed her jeans and knickers. The woman pushed her back on the mattress and a torch was shined on her vagina. Rough fingers examined her. "Virgin" she declared and allowed her up from the bed.

Next was Mariam. "Whore," declared the woman. Mariam was a virgin but with her friend Haniya she loved horse riding. The day her hymen split she had been shocked at the blood in her knickers. Her mother had reassured her some time later. Her friend had split her maidenhood while trying to use too large a tampon.

"Whore," shouted the woman on checking Haniya.

They were pushed from the tent and their status announced, "Two whores and a bride." The woman pushed Aleena forward.

The old man stepped forward and took hold of Aleena's arm pulling her towards him. It was clear that he was the commander of the group of fighters." I'll take this pretty one as my bride. Sort the other two between you."

The raping began right in the middle of the compound. Mariam's and Haniya's clothes were torn from them and they were held down, legs spread as the men queued to rape them. All three had been virgins and there was a scramble to be first when it was realised how inexperienced they were. The pain was unbelievable and the anal sex worse than the vaginal. It went on for hours. Bleeding and in pain the two girls were finally shoved into the tent.

They sat there clinging to each other, waiting for the next rape to come. They had their dream. They were now brides of the fighters. Aleena fared little better. The commander had taken her to a tent and fucked her arse and then her vagina. She was paralysed with shock as he pressed down on her. She remembered the rank smell of sweat that came from his body and the terrible stench that his breath had as he forced his tongue in her mouth.

She had been separated from her sister the next day, as the

Commander moved to another band of fighters to coordinate the attacks. She soon discovered that they were not the only girls to suffer the humiliation at the hands of the ISIS fighters. They would take the local women and use them as whores. Her position was slightly better in that she was the bride of the Commander. As a wife, she was just basically beaten and raped by the one man. It all changed within two weeks. Her "husband" was killed and she was then available to the rest of the group to rape as they pleased. She was not alone. She watched as they gang raped a girl no older than ten.

Chapter 9

It was around ten o'clock that the guests began arriving for the party at Benedict's apartment in Monaco. The first thing that struck the Driver as odd, was that there were about thirty young men and just two other couples. The females were introduced as Jane and Jill. While the men had drinks served at the bar, the two women disappeared into one of the bedrooms with Benedict's wife Mimi.

"Is this Adnan here yet?" asked the Driver.

Benedict looked round the room. "Not yet, but he will be."

Benedict left him holding a glass of champagne and went over to Jill and Jane's husbands. They rest of the male party goers gathered in small groups and seemed to say very little. It was the strangest party the Driver had ever attended. After about twenty minutes, Benedict and the spouses made their way to the room Mimi and her two friends had entered earlier. All eyes turned to the door.

The door opened and Benedict stepped into the room naked, "Party time."

The assembled men made their way to the room. Some began stripping naked while others just undid their flies and began rubbing their penises. The Driver made his way to the room and was at the back of the throng of naked and semi naked men. There were four swings suspended from the ceiling. They were not the type of swing that you see in the park but sex swings. The swing consisted of a chain connected to four leather straps that supported the four corners of a back support and straps in which the feet could be placed. Mimi, Jill and Jane were naked in three of the swings. Their feet were raised and strapped and their legs were widely spread showing their vaginas. "Who wants to fuck my slut wife?" shouted Benedict.

The men clustered around the three women and began fondling their breasts and pussies. "Come on somebody fuck me," shouted Mimi in encouragement. Somebody did fuck her followed by another somebody and then another. The three women seemed insatiable and seemed to have no bounds to their appetites. No orifice was off limits they sucked, they fucked and they buggered.

The Driver watched as the gangbang progressed, it was infectious. His penis was hard in his trousers and he reached down to rub it through the material. Benedict was watching his wife fucking as were the husbands of Jill and Jane. They were all naked and masturbating as they watched. After each successive participant had reached orgasm and deposited his sperm in Mimi's vagina, Benedict would kneel between her knees and lick the offering up.

The Driver, fully aroused, undressed and joined the queue to fuck Mimi. The form seemed to be fondle, fellatio then fuck, in an anti clockwise direction. The Driver was ready to come by the time it was his turn to fuck. He waited while Benedict cleaned up, then he entered her very wet and slippery vagina. To his surprise he was so excited by the whole experience that he came after just five or sex strokes. Mimi was continuously coming, clearly in a state of complete sexual ecstasy. He withdrew his penis and watched as his semen dripped from her shaved vagina. Benedict spoke before resuming his pussy cleaning duties.

"The man you need to speak to is fucking Jill now."

The Driver looked across to the next swing where a young Arab, in his late twenties, was pumping vigorously. It was distracting but he made a point of studying his face, so that he would recognise him with his clothes on.

It was an evening that the Driver would never forget. In a later conversation with Benedict, he had asked him if he minded his wife having sex with complete strangers.

"I knew Mimi had been in the sex trade when we met. She was quite open about being a prostitute. I, to my surprise found the whole idea stimulating. I think it is a combination of the voyeurism and the fact that she is so desirable to other men. It is hard to explain, but I enjoy watching her fuck and when the others have finished, knowing that she is mine."

"I am not sure I should like my wife to be doing it. That is of course, if I had a wife."

"We started talking about it first and Mimi suggested we went to the Naturist resort at cap D'Agde. It is a complete village where nudity is obligatory. At night the clubs are full of swingers from around the World. The clubs cater for every taste and there are no limits. We went and joined in at the clubs. I found I enjoyed it and Mimi really liked it. It just grew. "

The Driver was shocked but he could see no harm, his former employer was enjoying himself and he could not deny he had enjoyed fucking his wife.

Now dressed, he approached Adnan who was just buttoning his shirt. "I am the Driver," he said by way of introduction.

They left the apartment and the swinger's party and were in a hotel bar. Both were drinking coffee. Adnan spoke, "Mr Benedict says that you may be able to help us. We have shortages across the board. "

"It depends on what you want and where you want it."

"Manpads are an urgent requirement with the US, its allies and the Russians deploying air strikes across the region" Manpads, the Driver knew were manned, portable, air defence systems, or surface to air missiles, capable of being fired by a couple of fighters on the ground..

"Not cheap, fifty thousand a go, how many?"

"Three months for nine separate divisions, say a couple of thousand? "

"Double," said the Driver.

"What we ideally need to defend against air strikes is a self propelled surface to air system, something like the Russian Buk sustem."

"You are talking thirty million each."

"We have the money, do you have access to them?"

The truth was the Driver did not and had no idea where to get one. "Maybe, "he lied.

"Say three or four?"

The Driver was stunned. This was building to three hundred million dollars. "I am not sure that is possible."

Adnan rose from the seat. "I am disappointed. They said you were the man to go to."

The Driver just could not let the deal pass. "I will do it."

"Contact me when you have the order and we will help finalise payment and shipment. Benedict will be able to put you in touch. Don't let us down," he walked off into the night where a light drizzle had started to fall again.

Chapter 10

The Driver arrived at Moscow airport late in the evening. The rain seemed to be following him around the Globe, torrential in Argentina, continuous in London and Monaco and more of the same in Moscow. It was already dark when the taxi dropped him at the hotel. It was an old soviet built affair, not far from Red Square and looked like a grey sixties tower block, which is exactly what it was. Attempts had been made to spruce up the interior but it still had more the feel of a youth hostel than an hotel.

He had flown in from London and was on the trail of the armaments to fill Adnan's order for ISIS in Syria. Following their discussion in Monaco, Adnan had supplied his shopping list. It was clear that ISIS were expecting an all-out air attack down the road, anticipating that the Russians, having bombed Assad's governments immediate opposition, would team up with the Americans and their allies to go after them. Facing the prospect of the overwhelming air power, they needed a defence system.

Such systems had been purchased from the Russians in Venezuela and Iraq, but the Driver had no luck in finding a seller through his usual sources. He was looking for the Buk-M2E missile system. The Russians were the manufacturers and were unlikely to sell him the system to be used against their own strike force in Syria. So the usual channels were out. The one piece of information that had helped him in tracking down the system, was that he knew that it had been used in the Ukraine when a Boeing 777 Malaysian Airline flight had been downed. He had heard that an arms dealer, called Dovzhenko, had somehow gathered up four or five of the Buk-M2E series from the conflict, along with a stack of the generation 9

Grizzly missile racks, as part of the cover up and they were somewhere in the Crimea, or at least in the pro-Russian sector of the country.

He had set his sights on getting his hands on them, if they existed. The grizzly missiles were about seventy million each and the transporters and allied systems were a further twenty to thirty million. It was the deal of a lifetime, if he could source and supply them.

His search for Dovzhenko had led him to Moscow. He had met with him in London. He confirmed that he had the rocket launchers he sought but he had sold them. After money exchanged hands, Dovzhenko had given him an introduction to Lesta.

Now it was a matter of waiting.

The Driver woke early, went downstairs, ate and exited the hotel. He had checked his mobile phone was registered to a network and that itfunctioned. He sat in the lobby, constantly looking at his phone, waiting for the call but he realised that he had no way of knowing when Lesta would make contact. The waiting was interminable and he decided to get out for a bit of exercise. The walk to the shopping mall was shorter than he thought. He soon found himself in designer fashion paradise.

He was not exactly sure what the shopping arcade had been previously, but it had been transformed into shops that catered for the Russian rich and elite. It was clear that, while the sanctions imposed after the annexation of the Crimea were hitting the Country's economy badly, not all Russians were suffering equally.

Shop after shop, full of global brands, were displaying their goods. There was no shortage of customers and money was being spent. He lingered in a few shops to take up some time, but his mind was not on fashion and wandered to an exit after about an hour. He went through the doors and found himself in Red square.

The first thing that struck him was how unimpressive it was. Watching the May Day parades with the tanks, missiles and massed ranks of the Red army on television, he had expected it to be so much bigger. He walked to the centre and looked at the Podium over Lenin's Tomb. It was small, he wondered how the leaders of the country, their Polite Bureaux colleagues and all those generals, with their oversized caps, had managed to squeeze on it as the parade went by.

He made his way to the Tomb and joined the queue. The information told how the technicians had a whole laboratory devoted to preserving Lenin's body and they worked on the cutting edge of technology. He finally joined the slow walk past to view the glass encased, mortal remains of the former leader. He had to admit, it was a remarkable feat of preservation. The head did, however, look suspiciously like a Madam Tussaud's waxwork dummy. Suspending his scepticism, he left and went back onto Red Square.

The Square was populated with a group of street vendors and hawkers. They carried trays of goods, ranging from the ever present matryoshka dolls and fur hats, to ex-army watches and badges. The Driver was soon approached by the offer of an army watch, guaranteed to be waterproof to an incredible depth. Having avoided the temptation of buying the watch, he just observed the scene for a few moments.

The hawkers were, on closer inspection, a well organised group. Cars were parked off the square to supply the sellers. The car boots contained a vast array of fake and stolen goods aimed to be sold at inflated prices to the tourists. The street vendors were targeting the shoppers as they exited the luxury shopping centre.

Suddenly, a black van pulled up and discharged a group of leather coated police. The vendors ran, but those caught were beaten and dragged to a waiting van. It was brutal and swift. The owners of the outlets in the shopping centre obviously had little time for the competition and had paid the police to come and bang a few heads as a warning. He learnt later the raids were a regular affair and helped supplement the policemen's salaries.

Having exhausted the delights of Moscow's historic square, he returned to wait at the cheap hotel. He was tempted to move to the more international quarter, with its luxury accommodation and clubs. He decided keeping a low profile was the best strategy. Drawing attention to himself with a display of wealth was hardly advisable, given his mission was to source arms to be potentially used against the Russians in Syria. The iron curtain may have been drawn back. but the whole atmosphere of the country still had the feel of restrictions, surveillance and control. The suspicions surrounding foreigners was deeply ingrained in the psyche of the population.

He sat in the lobby looking at the television mounted in the lounge. There was a preponderance of programming showing positive images of Russian rural life and pictures and stories about the President. Even if he could have understood it, he guessed that daytime television here was a dull as dish water.

Eventually the phone rang. The voice was polite and enquired as to his journey and his health before proposing a meeting. His location ascertained, he was told to wait and he would be collected. Approximately twenty minutes later, the Mercedes pulled up outside and a Driver opened the rear door for him.

The drive through Moscow was interesting. There were vast swathes of grey tower blocks and pretty orthodox churches with their brightly painted exteriors and golden domes. The traffic was chaotic and it was clear that driving standards were appalling. Many Russians had never had a driving lesson in their lives and had merely bribed an official to issue them with a license, a cheaper option than paying for lessons. Once clear of the centre, they gained speed and soon arrived at a residence that was built to impress. The electronic gates opened and they passed the guards in the grounds.

He was shown into a large dining room with a table set for lunch. He was offered wine and a seat. Lesta appeared to great him. They sat and lunch began.

"You know Dovzhenko?" asked Lesta.

"Not really, I was in the market for something and he recommended you."

Lesta was being guarded. He did not know this man and he need to tread cautiously. "I am a banker. Is it perhaps a loan you seek?"

"That would be nice, but in truth I was hoping to buy some machinery."

There was silence as they ate. Lesta had tried to gain as much information as he could about the man he was sharing his table with. There was reassuring little to be found out about the Driver. He did know that he had worked with Hambros Benedict and that was a name that was known and trusted. "Tell me about Mr Benedict?"

The Driver realised that this was a test as to his credentials and his identity. It soon been clear that Lesta and Benedict's paths had crossed. The atmosphere between the two men lightened as each gained confidence in the other.

How can I help?" said Lesta.

The Driver pulled his shopping list from his pocket and placed it on the table between them. Lesta read in silence and stared long and hard at the man opposite. "This is a very expensive list. Can you afford it?"

There in lay the Driver's problem. Adnan had made it clear that ISIS would only pay on receipt of the goods in Syria and not before.

He would need to do the deal of his life if he was to pull it off. With Benedict's help, he could raise about seventy five million. He decided to be honest. "I am not sure. What do you have and what can you supply?"

"I can supply four Buks and an extra set of Grizzly missiles. For each, three hundred million dollars"

"Two hundred, I will pay fifty million as a deposit and the balance when I sell"

"You want me to trust you with a loan of one hundred and fifty million?" Lesta stayed calm showing no emotion, he had paid Dovzhenko nearly half of what was on the table. "I am sorry, I don't think we can do business;"

It was so close the Driver could taste it. "Two hundred and fifty million and seventy five down. That's my limit" He had agreed a price of what amounted to five hundred million dollars with Adnan. That would effectively turn his and Benedict's seventy five into two hundred and fifty million.

"You are responsible for transporting the goods from where they are, which is in the Crimea by the way. I will arrange the export licence outward, but you need to sort the end user certificates and onward transport."

"Agreed"

"I will arrange a line of credit for one hundred and seventy five million with a Bank, so you can pay me the full two hundred and fifty up front."

"What bank would lend an arms smuggler that sort of money?" The Driver was puzzled.

"Oh! Do not worry, it is called the Baltic Bank and I guarantee it is ready and waiting to do business with you."

Chapter 11

The Driver knew that he was playing for high stakes and his chance to bat in the major leagues. With the proceeds from this deal, he could be that step closer to not just being rich but part of the super rich. Now he had agreed his price with Lesta, he needed to sell on to Adnan and his ISIS chums. He was sitting at a table outside the Grand Bazaar in Istanbul. Adnan had texted the location from the airport when he had landed. Adnan was late, so he sat and sipped his coffee and people watched.

There was the usual motley crew of street vendors chasing Tourists and pickpockets plying their trade. For both, pickings were slim. The recent bombings and rise in state control were ensuring the downward trend in tourism was increasing. The rising rate of unemployment was having visible effects as well. Men were gathered on street corners waiting for casual labour or just smoking and talking. The influx of Syrian refugees had added to the pool of unskilled labour in the Country. Syrian boys as young as twelve would do the lowliest of jobs for a few pence a day. While the Government took vast sums from the EU, to prevent the refugees overwhelming the borders of the EU Countries with unwanted migrants, the camps in Turkey filled up with them.

A Syrian woman, dressed in the long black traditional dress, was making her way past a group of men standing by the corner of the alley, a few paces from where the Driver sat. They watched her progress, as she turned to pass them and go down the side road they started calling out racial abuse. It was clear that they had a real hatred and disgust for the woman. It seemed that the feeling was shared by the majority of the passers-by, who ignored the unfolding assault.

"Syrian whore," seemed the most popular insult the men employed as they pushed her from side to side. While brothels were legal and State sponsored in Turkey, the conservative government were steadily closing them down or driving them away from the centre. The prostitutes were licensed by the State and they were just not granting new permits to the sex workers, consequently the number available to the brothels were diminishing, so they had to close their doors. The biggest demand among Turkish men was for shemales, pre op transgender men and they were visible sitting on balconies in the old part of the town. The demand was, of course, still there for female prostitutes but the supply was diminishing. The Syrian women, in a bid to feed their families and with no work available for their husbands, were filling the gap.

The men were becoming increasingly abusive to the woman. "Like it up the arse?" one shouted to the encouragement of the others. Most of the sexual activity of the prostitutes, legal or illegal, centred on anal sex. The young Turkish men watched a diet of Western porn with the uninhibited porn stars being sodomised and apparently enjoying it. Their wives, more traditional and constrained, did not provide the service at home. The Syrian women were cheap and available but still denigrated.

The group of men had pulled the woman further back into the alley and were pulling at her clothes, grabbing her breasts and pushing their hands up her long gown, between her legs. The Driver wondered if he was to witness a rape over his coffee. It was clear that the police and passers- by had no intention of intervening and he certainly had no intention of drawing attention to himself. In any event, the Driver was not of a heroic disposition.

Matters came to a swift but violent conclusion. A young athletic man appeared and moving fast, with obvious combat training and almost balletic movements, broke noses and jaws. The man ran and the young man waved the Syrian woman on her way. The incident was over in a Split second, the Driver noted that he certainly would not want to be in the young man's bad books.

Adnan walk from the affray and sat down opposite The Driver. "Nice to see you again," he said, with no hint of breathlessness following his fight with the men. He had been watching the Driver at the table for some while when the assault on the woman had begun. He was a Syrian, had joined up to overthrow Assad. He had taken part in the demonstrations as a student, but become more and more of the opinion that there was something better in this life and had gravitated towards fundamentalist Islam. His aim now was the restoration of the Caliphate. Not a single country, but a Muslim area stewarded over by a single spiritual successor to the Prophet Muhammad.

"Impressive," said the Driver.

Adnan smiled, "Not really, I get quite a lot of practice."

There was a silence while the Driver looked for a way to broach the subject of arms selling. He called the waiter over and ordered two more coffees and sat back while they were made.

Finally, Adnan broke the silence, "Well?"

The Driver reached into his pocket and handed the specification across the table. He watched as Adnan's expression changed from one of mild impatience to disbelief. "You have this?"

The Driver nodded. His exterior calm covered the tension he felt. The price was now the issue. Would ISIS pay the figure he had in mind.

"How much?"

"Half a billion US dollars," the Driver said it matter of factly as though he was asking for payment of the weekly shopping bill in a supermarket.

Adnan's eyes widen and he let out a long slow breath. "When can we have them?"

"When can you pay?"

Adnan took a slow sip of his coffee and stared into the middle distance. The Driver felt his heart rate rise. This was the make or break. He waited trying to keep a poker face and betray none of the eagerness he was feeling. Finally, the silence was broken.

"We will pay your price, but there will be conditions." He paused and watched as The Driver's facial expression tried to remain impassive, but he knew that he was eager to do the deal, hungry in fact and greedy.

"What conditions?"

"Cash on delivery in Syria, once we have the goods we will transfer the money electronically. Secondly you organise the paper work and transport."

The Driver could not believe that his price had been accepted without argument. He had underestimated the need for ISIS missile defence against the US air attacks. If, and when the Russians were persuaded to work jointly with the Americans and target ISIS, the air assault would be devastating. The Grizzly missiles and the mobility the Buk-M2E system offered, would mean that ISIS would have a much better chance of prevailing.

The Driver knew that he had one big problem ,Turkey. Lesta could get the missiles out of the Crimea, given the right paper work. The Driver intended to obtain a purchase order from the Saudis and supply Lesta with it. He would then have to import the shipment into Turkey and truck it to the Syrian border. While he had connections with Saudi Arabia and knew their support for Al Qaeda, he had no contacts in Turkey.

He thought and decided that he had no alternative but to come straight out with it. "I have no contacts in Turkey. I need to truck the goods from Istanbul to the border. I cannot take the risk, I need the paperwork."

"We have the contacts. A man called Mehmet, he is head of Turkish Intelligence. He is a greedy and dangerous man but we have dealt with him many times. I will need to pay him, so I pay you less"

"How much less?"

"Two hundred million"

"That is ridiculous"

"So is your price."

The Driver was secretly overjoyed. The deal could not be better. He was putting up a mere seventy five million, the Baltic bank were lending him one hundred and fifty to pay Lesta and he would clear three hundred million before expenses, such as transport and bribes. His seventy five million would turn into a quarter of a billion dollars or more.

Both men shook hands and both men walked away happy. Now the hard work began. Adnan had to deal with Mehmet and The Driver had the Saudis to convince. Things were progressing nicely thought the Driver, as he sat in the taxi to the airport.

Chapter 12

Adnan had arrived two hours early for his meeting with Mehmet. The road, in which the Hamam or Turkish bath was, was in a busy area of the Faith district, making it easy to merge with the shoppers. He had met Mehmet, the deputy head of the security service, on two previous occasions and he had nothing but dislike for the man. He had no choice but to do business with him, but there was always an element of uncertainty in the outcome.

The Turkish attitude towards the more fundamental Islamic movement was mixed and often contradictory. Whist along with the Kurds, ISIS was branded a terrorist organisation, the more fundamentalist views it propounded to were closer to the Governments more reactionary beliefs than to the secularism line promulgated in the Country. It was also an elite divide, the more wealthy, looking to maintain the secularism in which they thrived, while the poorer mass of the population were looking for change. The conflict over the Kurdish homeland also added confusion to the mix. The Government was not averse to using ISIS as an excuse to cover their attacks on the Kurds.

The background tension within Turkey made Adnan's position and relationship with Mehmet precarious. There was no doubt that he would take a bribe if it suited him, but in the final analysis he would put Turkish interest first. Adnan was banking on the fact that a fully armed ISIS in Syria served Turkey's aims. Tensions between Turkey and the Russians were high after the shooting down of a Russian aircraft that had flown into Turkish airspace. The conflict between ISIS and the Kurds was also not unappealing to the Turks.

Adnan had arrived early to see if any form of trap was being set to take him. If it suited Mehmet, he was quite capable of using the capture of a high ranking commander to further himself or curry favour with his superiors. He had scouted the baths and surrounding area and was fairly confident that today was not the day Mehmet was going to take him prisoner.

As he watched the entrance to the baths, situated between two small shops, he was curious to see two young men kissing just behind the narrow arch that lead to the entrance. Whist homosexuality was not a crime, a public display such as this was highly unusual and risky. One of the men continued to the baths and the other walked off and disappeared into the crowd.

Adnan did one last circuit of the immediate area and headed inside to the bathhouse. The outside had seen better days and could have done with some renovation work, but the domed interior with its columns rising to the roof was splendid. He underessed and placed his clothes in the full length lockers. The young man he had seen kissing his lover outside was busying himself assembling oils and towels, ready for his massage duties.

He waited outside the bathing area for Mehmet's arrival. He arrived exactly at the appointed time. They acknowledged each other and proceeded to the washing, scraping and steaming ritual. The baths had been a meeting place for socialising and business since the Ottomans. Adnan and Mehmet were following an age old tradition as they sat to discuss matters.

"We need clearance to move some goods from Istanbul to the Syrian border." Adnan reached the point of their meeting after exchanging pleasantries.

"What sort of goods?"

"Let's call it humanitarian aid."

"Let's not. Why don't you tell me, exactly what you want me to allow into Syria."

Adnan was fairly sure that Mehmet did not give a flying fuck what went into Syria as long as it posed no risk to Turkey and lined his pocket in the process. The issue was that if Mehmet knew the cargo, would he adjust the price accordingly? He tried to obscure the exact contents of the convoy," Ammunition, light arms and medical supplies."

"How many trucks?"

"Nine or ten"

"Now here is an odd thing. As you may know I operate an intelligence network and it is telling me something different. Now how would you account for that?" said Mehmet.

Adnan was beginning to feel that this was not going to be a cheap day. The Driver had extracted a very full price for the missile systems and now it looked like safe passage was going to add to the tally. "You obviously have your answers, so shall we move to the price?"

"My sources tell me that at least three or four of the trucks will need to be extra wide. To me that suggests something very big, but more to the point, something very expensive. Am I right?"

Adnan nodded and knew the price was rising by the sentence.

Mehmet smiled, "Well I think fifty thousand a truck. Call it half a million dollars."

Adnan was shocked, that was five times more than he anticipated. He now had a dilemma. Did the man sitting in the towel in front of him really know what he was transporting or was he fishing. "That is a crazy number," he said.

Mehmet sat silent for a while. He too was trying to gauge the value of the load. He was a good reader of men. He had not risen so far without the ability to see if someone was lying. "I think it is a reasonable number given what you want me to let pass." He was bluffing. The only information he had was from some haulage contractors who had been in discussions with an Englishman. He was not even sure that the two were connected.

"Two hundred and fifty thousand," said Adnan.

Mehmet knew his hunch was right. If he had said ten thousand a truck he would have accepted it was food and small arms, but to offer that sort of money, he knew Adnan had something far more valuable to ISIS than a few automatic rifles.

"Half a million or your trucks won't leave the quayside."

Adnan knew he was outmanoeuvred. "Ok. But we will only pay when we cross the border"

"I think not. You have ten days to put the money in this account." He removed a card from the small bag he had beside him in which he had his keys, phone and wallet.

Adnan took the card and holding on to it got up to leave. Mehmet spoke again. "Won't you join us for a bit of fun and games?" He indicated the young gay man Adnan had seen kissing earlier.

"I think you have shafted me once and I think that is enough for one day."

Mehmet could not help but laugh as he made his way to the private massage room with the young man.

Chapter 13

The Driver received the news from Adnan that the way was clear for the transit of his cargo across Turkey from Istanbul to the Syrian border. He now needed an export license to move the goods from the port of Sevastopol in the Crimea and across the Black Sea to Istanbul

The political situation of the Peninsular presented its own challenges. In 2014 the Crimea and Sevastopol became part of the Russian Federation following the annexation of the territory and a dubious referendum held under Russian military supervision. However the European Union, most nations and the United Nations still consider Crimea and Sevastopol to be part of Ukraine

The Driver knew that there was a real danger in exporting arms from the region. Sanctions existed and even without them, the Russians were not likely to allow the export of rocket launchers that may be used by ISIS against the Russian air force in Syria. The solution was Saudi Arabia.

The Driver needed an order from the Saudi government to satisfy the export requirements to ship the missiles from the Crimea. Pressure in Britain, which had been selling vast amounts of weapons to the Saudis, was building to stop the trade. Human rights violations and the active support by the Saudis of dissident groups in the Yemen and all over the region were beginning to raise concerns. The US had stopped supplying the Saudis with arms and Britain had stepped in to fill the gap. Momentum was gathering among the Members of Parliament in the UK to stop the trade. Time may well be running out for the Driver to use the Saudi route to acquire the documentation.

He had no choice, so he found his way to the Saudi Defence Attaché's Office in Queen's Gate, South Kensington. Lesta had provided him with a contact name and after many phone calls, he had his appointment.

"How may we help?" said the attaché.

Now the Driver faced the dilemma on how to proceed. Walking in off the street and asking for fake documentation to deliver arms to an Al-Qaeda group in Syria was unlikely to be viewed with anything less than total suspicion and ignored.

"The matter is delicate and complicated," he began. "Some friends, who are engaged in bringing freedom abroad, have asked me to help them in their endeavours"

There was silence. The attaché merely sat and waited for him to continue. He had no choice but to go on. "The have requested that I organise the shipment of some essential equipment to further their ambitions."

The Attaché smiled and tilted his head to one side. "Where would these friends be?"

The Driver felt less than confident in his next statement, "Syria."

"I am not sure that is anything to do with us. I think you'll find that this is the Saudi Defence Office and the clue is in the sign over the door as you enter, Defence."

The Driver sat and squirmed. He had no idea how to proceed in the matter." I think I may be wasting your time. My close friends Nizar and Adnan gave me the impression that your government might be sympathetic to their plight?"

"Please wait." He stood up and left the room. The Driver was left sitting uncomfortably looking at the walls for nearly an hour, before the door re-opened and the attaché entered and resumed his seat.

"Sorry for the delay. You were saying?"

The Driver was not at all sure what he was saying and did consider leaving before he dug himself in too deep. He half feared that the time he had been left twiddling his thumbs had been used to contact MI5 to organise his arrest and interrogation when he set foot on the pavement outside.

"I was saying that I have some friends in Syria who are struggling for supplies and need a little help to withstand the Russian air threat to their homes and people."

"These supplies wouldn't be by any chance Buk-M2E systems, would they?"

The Driver's mouth dropped open in surprise.

"We are not fools. We do have our own intelligence network around the World. We like to know what is going on with our friends as well as our enemies."

"Sorry, I am out of my area of expertise and out of my usual sphere of business," said the Driver.

"Clearly," he said. "But, as you may have gathered, we are not unsympathetic to the plight of our brothers in foreign lands. The problem we have is that we are under intense international pressure over our involvement in the Yemen. There is a report due here in the UK detailing doubts, regarding the weapons the British had have been selling us and where they end up. They fear what we buy today may well be used against them tomorrow. We have to tread carefully. You understand?"

The Driver nodded. He sat in silence. It was clear that the interconnectivity of the various terrorist groups was far deeper than he had realised. The links to each other and governments were a complex web that spanned the Middle East. The Saudis knew about his deal, but the question was would they provide him with the official order signed by them to allow him to move his product from Russia to Turkey?

"I am not trying to create tension here. There is a genuine decision to be made as the stakes are high, not only for your friends but also for us. You want an order from us to allow you to move these rockets from Russian Federal territory. We on the other hand want to maintain good relations with the UK. In that it is highly likely down the road, our mutual friends will be bringing down, not only Russian planes with these missiles, but also British and American ones as well. You understand that such an important decision needs consideration?"

The door opened and the Driver looked up in anticipation, only to be confronted with a man brining in coffee and biscuits.

The wait seemed interminable as he was left alone, yet again. Lunchtime came along with more coffee and sandwiches. He could do nothing however but wait. He read all the newspapers and resorted to looking for games to play on his mobile phone as he sat alone in the office. He found that he was far too distracted and agitated to concentrate on Angry Birds and gave up the effort.

Finally, after nearly six hours, with the time approaching half past seven in the evening, the door opened and the Attaché came in dressed in a dinner jacket. "Embassy reception, doing my James Bond impression," he said by way of explanation.

The Driver smiled politely. "You look very smart."

"Thank you, flattery will get you everywhere." He placed a white envelope on the table. "You have your order, good luck."

Chapter 14

While the Driver was making progress obtaining the necessary documents, loans and organising the transport for the missile launchers and missiles racks from the Crimea to Turkey, Adnan and Nizar found it was a case of one step forward and two steps back.

"Are you telling me that we have just paid the bastard Mehmet and the fucker has gone and got himself killed? How the fuck did he manage that, he is surrounded by his two goons even when he takes a shit?" said Adnan.

Nizar looked out of what was once the window of the partly demolished house, onto the completely demolished surrounding buildings. The atmosphere was laden with dust being whipped up by the early morning breeze. He watched as a mini tornado was created as it eddied between the piles of rubble. On days like this, he did wonder why he had come to this shit hole. He had a good middle class upbringing in the UK and had done well enough at school to get him into Leicester University. He had always been interested in the wild life and loved his trips to the zoo, where his parents had taken him on as a child. Getting into Leicester had seemed to fulfil his dream. After all, it even had a building named after the supremo of wild life filming, David Attenborough.

He had not even been a particularly devout Muslim and had partied away his first year fully immersing himself in student life. Then he had felt guilty after a particularly heavy week of hedonism and felt the urge to attend the Mosque. It had grown from there. The Imam and the new group of friends showed him the way. The West was conspiring against Islam and the murder of his Muslim brothers in the Middle East and they started to change his perceptions. It was as if a great truth had been revealed to him and eventually he just left the University to begin his training in Afghanistan. Now nine years later he was in Syria leading the fighters of ISIS.

"He was killed in a bath house along with the masseur, he was fucking," said Nizar.

"You are fucking kidding me? I was there with him when we met. He wanted a threesome, with him and his little friend. I saw that masseur kissing his boyfriend outside the Hamam before I went in to meet Mehmet. Was it the boyfriend, jealousy?"

"That is how it looks on the face of it but it seems we had him executed." said Nizar.

"We had him executed? Why did we do that?"

"Not we, specifically, me. I put a hit on him when I was in Iraq. The bloke you saw kissing the masseur was a hit man just known as Annubis. Mehmet had been in London shooting Jihadis a week or so before and killed my brother. I was so pissed off at Mehmet that I put a contract out on him."

"Fucking great, we are bribing him to let our weapons into Syria and you are paying some fucker to have him killed. That has got to be the most expensive, stupid thing we have done in a while. I am pissed off. I am really fucking pissed off."

"I would never have guessed if you hadn't told me," said Nizar. "I was in Iraq. I had no idea what you were up to here. I would still have had the scumbag killed though."

"Well what to do we do now? We have half a billion dollars worth of launchers and missiles turning up in Istanbul and no guarantee what will happen when they unload."

Nizar had to admit it was a mess and had not a clue as to what to do now. Mehmet had been their only reliable contact. The flip flop policy of the Turkish Government towards ISIS and Al- Qaeda just made the task of dealing with Turkish officials unpredictable.

"Can we approach his boss or his replacement?"

"His boss is not a goer, he has had family killed in Turkey by a bombing we instigated and hates our cause. Do you know Mehmet's replacement?"

Nizar knew that they had no idea or relationship with the new security chief, "No not really."

"We are fucked aren't we? What do I tell the Driver? "Sorry about this. But could you, shove a pile of rockets up your arse and smuggle them, across Turkey to Syria, without anybody noticing?"

Nizar laughed despite himself.

"It's not funny," said Adnan

"I know, but what can we do? Realistically, there is nothing we can do."

"We need those missiles. There is no doubt that once the Russians have solidified Assad's position they will turn on us. We are getting off lightly as the Americans and the Russians are not cooperating, but when it suits the Russians they will work with the rest of the coalition forces to blow the shit out of us. Then Assad will be left with a vice like grip on the Country and go to the negotiating table in an overwhelmingly strong position."

"Look the deal with the Driver is cash on delivery, so if he can't get them across the border into Syria we don't lose any money."

"No but we lose the fucking war," said Adnan.

Chapter 15

While things were moving slowly for the Driver, as he brought the threads of the biggest arms deal he had ever done together in London, Tim Burr was feeling very happy today as he walked through the lobby into Thames House, the home of MI5. The work was interesting and the people pleasant, which was a change from his previous post at the Paris Embassy. The icing on the cake was his relationship with Jackie and her young son Daniel. They had just meshed from the beginning and when he moved in with her it all came together. He felt like he was part of something, a proper family.

Full of the joys of spring he bounded up the stairs to his office. He passed Jeff Stiles on the stairs. "Are you still on for a drink after work tonight?"

"If you are buying then I am on."

"Would you double check with Elaine to see if she is still coming?"

"I am just on my way to see her now. I shall remind her."

Tim settled into his morning's work but was too excited to fully concentrate. Stiles, true to his word, was sitting in Elaine Wilkins' office drinking coffee. It was a Friday and they liked to have their weekly meeting and review their progress. Elaine would update the Home Secretary later that day. The current Home Secretary was keen on face to face. His predecessor liked everything in his in box, so he could read it, at his leisure.

"Don't forget Tim's drinks party in the American bar tonight. He is threatening Champagne all round and he is bringing his girlfriend."

"Have you met her before?"

"Oh yes, several times. She is very attractive and has a personality unusual for an accountant."

"Accountant, I didn't know that. Not a profession you associate with interesting. "

"No, she is really pleasant and doing well. She has just made partner and Tim tells me that she has picked up a massive audit of a Bank. To be precise the Baltic Bank, I did allude to them over that surprise lunch you bought me at the Savoy. I don't suppose you have any more cancelled lunch appointments I could help you out with again?"

"That was a one off, we can't keep blowing the tax payers money on wining and dining, we are not MPs you know. I don't remember you mentioning the Baltic Bank though?"

"Perhaps I didn't. It was sort of peripheral to a bit of dodgy arms supplying to ISIS and the possibility of weapons being used here following the Paris attacks."

"I am not clear. What has a bank got to do with arms?"

"I am not sure but the Bank seems to be under the control of a few Russians that the Americans are interested in, money laundering and a bit of state plundering of their Countries assets. They want to have a crack at seizing their ill-gotten gains and ramp up the pressure on Russia. Hitting people in the pocket usually gets their attention."

"I am pretty sure that I told you to drop it now I recall."

"You did, but I like to keep a watching brief. If they help ISIS move money about in the West then sooner or later that will translate into bombs and guns on the streets in the UK. I am just keeping an eye on them that is all."

Elaine looked down at her shoes and wondered if they really did match her suit. She came to the conclusion that they didn't, which was a shame as they were actually comfortable. Notwithstanding that, she knew that as soon as Stiles left she would have to change them. She had about twenty possible alternatives in the cupboard in her office. "Look I know you can't leave a thing alone once you start and I appreciate this obsessiveness is the very thing that makes you so effective, but I do need you to take my instructions occasionally."

Stiles looked out the window avoiding her gaze, he knew that she was unhappy about his decision to keep looking at the Baltic Banks activities, but his gut instinct meant that he felt compelled to keep a watching brief on events. While he couldn't prove it, he knew that the Bank was up to no good and that made him concerned for Tim and in particular Jackie. The gaining of the Bank's audit had been the final push she needed to make partner. Tim had told him about the struggle she had had to qualify as an Accountant. Her first husband had been one of the controlling, wife bashing varieties. With no support and with a young child, she had made her advancement in the profession entirely on her own.

Whilst she was doing well, there is nothing like bringing in new business and fee income to boost partnership prospects. Tim had told him how she had had a real stroke of luck when a close friend, who had qualified with her, had landed the Finance Director's role at the Bank in Iceland. He had not forgotten his friend and steered the audit her way, despite stiff competition from the big boys in the accountancy profession to get their hands on it. It was almost unheard of for a banking audit not to go to the Big Four, as they were known. The gaining of the audit sealed her promotion.

Stile's interest in the Baltic bank, therefore, had a very personal element to it, he had no intention of taking his eye off it. He, his wife and daughter, who was roughly the same age and Daniel, Jackie's son, had become very firm friends over the last few months. They had shared dinners, theatre trips and theme park days out together.

"Of course, I always listen in the end," he said to placate Elaine.

The subject changed, she was finally up to speed and ready for her meeting with the Minister. "What time are we expected tonight?"

"Seven thirty-ish"

The American Bar at the Savoy had served drinks to patrons that ranged from royalty to film stars. Tonight it was serving drinks to a bunch of accountants and MI5 staff. Tim pulled Jackie towards him and gave her a big hug as their guest arrived.

They made do with house champagne and the nibbles that were handed out as a matter of course by the bar staff. The bar was relatively empty. The pianist was just starting his first set, playing a "Nightingale Sang in Barclay Square. "

Time made sure that everyone was present and had their glass full before calling for attention.

"Welcome friends new and old, I know most of you will have guessed why you are her?"

"You've won the lottery and are going to give us a million quid a piece," called out a voice.

"More like he's going to run the London Marathon and wants us to sponsor him for a hundred apiece."

"None of those," said Tim waving his arms to settle the hubbub. "Jackie and I are getting married and you are all invited."

"I knew it would cost us money somewhere along the line," called a voice. Amid the laughter the couple were toasted and congratulated. The pianist played the wedding march followed by the funeral march as a joke.

"Jeff, I would really appreciate if you would be my best man?" said Tim.

"I would love to. Are you sure, we have only been friends for a short time?" said Stiles.

"Of course I am. After all you are the man that saved my life from the homicidal Turk, Mehmet, in Wood Green."

"We all make mistakes," said Stiles.

"And," said Tim, "you don't know enough to embarrass me with the Best Man's Speech"

Chapter 16

The Driver sat looking out across the bay at Sevastopol and let out a long deep breath. It had been a long few days trying to deal with the paperwork involved in exporting his cargo to Turkey. The weather was unseasonably warm. The sweeping bay was as calm as a pond and the water a deep blue. The pigeons lined up along the wall and waited for the tourists to feed them. It was hard not to notice the large Russian naval presence with the war ships dominating the harbour and the coming and goings of the tenders. He had no idea why the fleet was in, or if it was a constant feature.

The enormity and vulnerability of his financial position was beginning to sink in, as he watched a young couple taking photos of each other, with the bay as a backdrop. There were so many ifs that he had chosen to ignore. The overriding concern was, obviously, the massive debt he would owe if any part of the operation went wrong. Owing one hundred and seventy million dollars to a group of Russian oligarchs, even if the loan was ostensibly through a bank, was something most rational people would endeavour to avoid. The Baltic Bank was and he knew it, no more than a front to launder money for the mobsters of Russia. This bank would not be going through the Courts for a repossession order in the case of a default, it would be making funeral arrangements for the errant debtor.

The first major hurdle he had faced was physically moving the Buks. Driving them through the centre of town and up to the docks had never been on the cards. He had managed to organise the hire of two low loaders to transport them. The people were, however, used to military hardware moving down to the Russian naval base and the transporters attracted less attention than would have been expected. The fact that he could only get his hands on two loaders meant the trip had to be repeated a second time. The first hurdle was overcome, the launchers and containers containing the Grizzly missiles were dockside.

The unusual nature and shape of the cargo had, in itself, presented numerous problems. Normally to transport containers, he would merely contact his shipbroker and the matter would be handled for him. The broker would find a ship and obtain a price for taking the cargo from A to B. Transporting a complete mobile ground to air missile system four times over had presented the broker with a unique set of problems. Endless back and forth communication had taken place over health and safety and terrorist threats. Understandably, the ship owners had concerns over their ship blowing up or being attacked.

Matters had finally been resolved and he travelled to the Ukraine to ensure that it went without a hitch. Watching the tourists and people having their lunch, over looking the sea, he finally felt optimistic that the cargo would sail and arrive in Istanbul. All was aboard and the ship was about to sail. He was still concerned, but felt confident that the first stage was complete as he got up and prepared to fly to Istanbul to meet the ship on its arrival.

He would have felt a lot more concern if he had known what was transpiring in Moscow.

Lesta had just received news of a concerning nature and had managed to arrange a meeting with a contact at the Kremlin. Unlike the Crimea the rain was pouring down as he entered the lobby of the hotel.

"Volkov, it is so nice to see you," the bureaucrat rose and shook Lesta's hand.

Lesta sat and ordered coffee "Please tell me what the problem is,

Mikael?"

He paused before responding to Lesta. He wondered how to approach the matter. He knew that the man sat before him was closely connected to the Kremlin, he needed to be careful in delivering the message, "It is a delicate matter and I say, before I commence, that it may be a matter of the left hand not knowing what the right is doing. So if you are not involved, I do hope you will not be offended?"

"You know me. I am not easily upset and it is better to have things out on the table."

Mikael suspected that that might not be strictly the case and that Lesta and his associates had quite a reputation for bodies turning up around the place if they failed to achieve their goals. In any event he had no choice but to broach the matter." Do you know a chap called Dmytro Dovzhenko?"

Lesta of course knew, Dovzhenko, had just a few months before, spent over a million dollars buying rocket launchers from him. The same launchers and missiles he had sold on to the Driver, "The name sounds familiar."

"I will try and refresh your memory. Dovzhenko is, well was, a small time arms dealer emanating from the Ukraine. He started off selling bits and pieces left behind when the Soviet Republic started to fragment. He then became a contractor, used in the dismantling and disposing of surplus military hardware. He was a sort of scrap metal dealer, but scraping decaying and dangerous weapons that had been left to rot, and not cars."

"I know of him," said Lesta.

"You may recall that there was an incident involving the shooting down of an international airliner over the Ukraine. The incident was traced back to us, or at least to Russian missiles. The situation was very tense and confused at the time. There was a distinct possibility of all out war between the loyalist Russians in the east of the Ukraine and the Western backed rest of the Country. We began moving armaments into the Ukraine in readiness. The war failed to materialise and the West went for the usual sanctions."

"I don't see what this has to do with me or this Dovzhenko?"

"The Crimea held a referendum and joined the Russian federation. Thinking that there may be some sort of Western response, in particular targeted air strikes on Russian held bases in the Peninsula, we moved in four mobile rocket launcher systems in readiness for a NATO or European response."

"Seems a sensible course of action," said Lesta.

"Of course, except that left the launchers in the Crimea, and more to the point, what can be described as the smoking gun. Sitting there is the very launcher and missiles that in effect committed the war crime of blasting a jet out of the sky, killing innocent passengers. Having denied the very existence of these weapon systems ever being deployed by us in the Ukraine, four of them sitting there, as plain as the nose on your face would be, to say the least, a bit awkward."

Lesta was himself feeling a bit awkward, having just bought and sold the very same launchers which were currently being shipped off to Syria and very likely down the road would be used against the Russian air force. "I can see that would be difficult."

"It would be a massive loss of face for the Government to have the non-existent missiles turning up. So that is where Dovzhenko came in. He was paid to destroy and scrap the evidence. He was paid handsomely to do this with discretion."

Lesta's brain was working rapidly, weighing his options. What he said in the next few minutes might have severe consequences, both financially and health wise. On the one hand, he was not overly happy at losing the money he had paid Dovzhenko for the missile launchers and the profit he would make from the Driver. On the other hand, he was not keen on pissing off the Kremlin, which would be a definite death sentence.

The bureaucrat continued. "It would appear that Mr Dovzhenko decided to take the money to destroy the evidence and then not do so, preferring instead to sell the launchers on. Sadly Mr Dovzhenko is no longer with us and had no time to even spend the money. Life is very unpredictable and tenuous. Death can take us all without warning. Don't you agree?"

Lesta got the message loud and clear and decided to confirm his part in the affair. "I was not aware of this and I bought the systems from Dovzhenko in good faith. In fact, I was more doing him a favour. He was struggling with the storage costs."

"Of course, an act of selfless generosity on your part"

"Exactly so."

"And what are you going to do, now that you are aware of the facts?"

"What do you want me to do?"

"As a good Russian and friend of the Kremlin, we would expect that these embarrassing items just disappeared"

Lesta was beginning to squirm. "That may prove a little difficult. I have sold them on you see."

"Oh dear, that is indeed a little difficult. To whom, may I ask have you sold them?"

"To an arms dealer known as the Driver"

"Where are they now?"

"They are heading for Syria." Lesta was now really beginning to feel uncomfortable. "I have no means of stopping them."

After a long pause while the bureaucrat contemplated the situation before speaking "We do, however, have the means to stop them."

Chapter 17

The Drivers' cargo had arrived in Turkey at the terminal in Haydarpaşa at the Southern entrance to the Bosphorus and that is where it looked like it was destined to remain.

"Why did you let me get it here if you didn't have the paper work?" he was shouting down the phone to Adnan.

"The paper work was organised, but unfortunately our contact making the arrangements was murdered."

"But I am fucked. I have your goods sat on the dockside and the only reason it has not been seized is that I managed to get the paper work for onward transmission to Saudi Arabia. What the fuck am I supposed to do? Ship it to the Saudis and ask them if they would ship it back so it can be stuck here again?"

Adnan could hear the desperation in the Drivers' voice but had no solution. "I am sorry, get the cargo to Syria as agreed and we will pay you."

The Driver slumped to the ground on the dockside and sat staring at the activity on the quayside. He needed a miracle if he was to walk away alive from this one. The one hundred and seventy five million dollars was due to be re-paid to the Russians in under a week. The clock was ticking to his death.

He could run and hide, but they would find him in the end and it would only end one way. These were not the kind of people that let you default. The situation was hopeless. He had phoned Benedict to see if he had any suggestions. The conversation had gone badly.

Faced with the loss of the twenty five million he had put into the venture, he was less than impressed that the Driver had not foreseen the possibility of a hiccup in Turkey. He had rightly accused the Driver of not being hands on enough. He should have organised the paperwork in Turkey himself rather than entrusting it to some Jihadi, as Benedict referred to Adnan.

The Driver knew that Benedict was right. He had cut corners to get the deal done, in his eagerness to get in the big time money he was now facing the consequences. Relying only on one individual, Mehmet, had always been risky. His death had been unforeseeable, but he should have insisted on a belt and braces approach, a back-up, or that he had the necessary paperwork before the cargo left Sevastopol. This was all easy with hindsight, but now, too late to be wise.

He looked up to see the trucks arriving. The four Volvo loaders lined up with the two accompanying, covered articulated vehicles. An elderly Turk got out from the lead truck and wandered over to him. The other drivers gathered in a group talking, waiting for instructions. The driver spoke English, "Call me Jazz," he said, "are we ready to load?"

"Your English is very good?"

"That's what you get if you live somewhere for ten years. They deported me eventually, but not before I had made enough to buy a truck when I got back and start in the haulage business," he smiled. "So what's up?"

"No paper work, we are stuck on the docks on bond."

"Well you have paid for the trucks and the drivers. So either way I am a happy man. Shall I go or do you want to load?"

He was right he had paid for the trucks and the labour. "Load them up."

The trucks were loaded and sitting on the quayside as darkness fell. Their drivers sat around in the trucks eating or playing cards. The Driver had tried everything he knew to get the cargo out of the docks. He could neither bribe, nor talk his way out. It was an impasse and only a matter of time before customs seized the shipment.

One of the men listening to the radio in his cab, jumped from the vehicle and rushed across to the Driver and Jazz. An excited conversation followed and the whole crew ran to turn on radios.

The Driver followed Jazz to the radio, now turned up full volume. "What is it?"

"A coup, the army is trying to seize control. Parliament attacked the bridges in Istanbul, across the Bosphorus, are barricaded with tanks."

The drivers began to run from the docks leaving the trucks unattended, "Where are they going?"

"To their families," replied Jazz. In the end, two drivers and Jazz remained listening intently to the news reports, with Jazz periodically translating. It appeared that a faction of the army had broken away and, calling themselves The Peace at Home Council, were attempting to overthrow the President and gain control. The coup was taking place in the capital, Ankara, and Istanbul.

Chaos reigned while the President was on holiday in Marmaris, in the south of the country. He had avoided capture and was organising the counter attack. For a while it looked as if the rebels would succeed, but the balance of the army remained loyal and the President was slowly organising the counter insurgence.

Jazz's mobile rang and was answered. The conversation seemed frenzied and almost hysterical to the Driver. Jazz was almost crying and shouting at the same time. He put the phone down.

"I must go," he said and ran to the articulated truck and began to uncouple the cab from the trailer. The other drivers stood around confused.

"What is happening?" shouted the Driver as he physically retrained the semi hysterical Turk,

"The coup has failed and my son is trapped with his tank crew by the mob. I need to get his wife and my grandchildren and get away before they are taken."

The Driver thought, "I have a plan, Listen we can make use of the confusion to save your son and move my missiles."

The other crew members had fled the docks leaving Jazz and the Driver on their own. The Dock entrance was unguarded and they drove the Buk, complete with its rack of missiles, off the loader. They had removed the trampoline from the Buk exposing the vehicle in its full glory. It was an imposing piece of military hardware as it sped from the dockyard.

Jazz was constantly on the phone to his son and army buddies. His son was a Colonel and was guaranteed to die in the post coup crackdown, as were those under his command. Their only hope was to get out of Turkey. The Drivers' skill in driving soon came into its own and he soon had the launcher trundling north to the city. Trying to come south, in a truck, were Jazz's son and six rebels, their three wives and four children.

"They have been stopped by loyalist forces," said an almost crying Jazz.

As they rounded a bend, they could see in the headlights a truck surrounded by a group of soldiers. The Driver stopped. "Listen to me and get a grip." He made sure that the Turk understood and then he started the Buk and drove towards the road block

He waited in the cab while the soldiers stared open mouthed at the massive rocket launcher. Jazz began to speak to the Major in charge of the road block. The Driver noticed that there was a lot of arm waving and milling about. The young officer in charge got onto his mobile, there was more milling and arm waving. Then the truck with Jazz's son and the other soldiers, wives and children was allowed to pass. The Driver turned the Buk and they made their way back to the dockyard.

The dockyard was unguarded as the Driver and the truck drove back to the quayside. They stopped the convoy. After a brief introduction the soldiers loaded the Buk back onto the loader. Wives and children were boarded and the convoy set off on the road to the Syrian border.

"It worked, I can hardly believe it. Thank you," said Jazz as he drove the truck.

The soldiers were all for arresting Jazz's son and his fellow deserters when the missile launcher had arrived. In fact they did not even know that the Turkish army owned such a missile system so their surprise has been twofold. Jazz had interrupted proceedings by thanking God that the crew had arrived to operate the launcher.

He explained that the Buk was to be moved to the border to defend the Country against possible Russian or Syrian air strikes. Their President feared that in the chaos their enemies would use the opportunity to take advantage of their weakness. He and the Driver, who had remained in the darkness of the cab of the Buk, were just mechanics and had orders to ready the launcher and had gone in search of the crew to man. It.

The soldiers blocking the road were suspicious but none was sufficiently senior to countermand a direct order, perhaps from the President making his way back to restore order. The major had phoned a superior and explained he had detained a Colonel his men and a mobile ground to air missile launcher. The General on the other end of the phone knew nothing of this capability, but again, assuming that the reason for that was the sensitive nature of it, that was understandable. He also had no desire to interfere with the air defence system of the Country and had given the go ahead for Jazz's son and his fellow rebels to be let go.

The Driver had done it. He was driving his cargo to Syria. It had taken a failed coup d'etat, a deported Turk, his son and half a dozen deserters, their wives and children, but he was on his way.

Chapter 18

The road to the border between Turkey and Syria was closed and the Drivers convoy came to a halt. The Lorry Park was crammed with vehicles and he and his motley mix of deserters, wives and children settled down to a make shift meal. The attempted coup had failed and the country was completely under control and the arrests had begun. The leaders of the coup were first, but the government used the failed attempt to crack down on all possible opposition to its regime. Colleges were closed, teachers arrested and, for some unknown reason, so were the vast majority of judges.

The border was chaos with no one clear as to what was happening. On the Syrian side there was a steady stream of refuges fleeing the conflict, hoping for a better life further west. On the Turkish side there was a sea of humanitarian aid from the various countries in Europe. Some were vast, twenty or thirty trucks, others just consisted of a local effort of just one small lorry.

The Driver knew that he could not stay in this impasse situation but could see no immediate way of crossing into Syria. The soldiers had discarded their uniforms in an attempt to avoid capture but, lacking documentation, their prospects of escaping the purge taking place seemed remote.

An English voice could be heard in the hubbub of the humanity, vehicles crowded together waiting to cross. "Two of the trucks for fuck sake! Don't we have enough problems stuck in this shit hole?"

He wandered in the direction of the raised voices out of curiosity to see a convoy plastered in red crosses. The problem was immediately apparent. One truck, looking like it had been built when Noah was riding the flood, had its bonnet raised and steam issuing from the radiator. The other, not much of an earlier vintage, had a total collapse of the rear suspension.

"That seems well and truly buggered," said the Driver to the angry Englishman..

"That's a bleeding understatement. I can't fucking believe it, I get all this way and then the bloody things give up on me, just as we are about to get into Syria. He introduced himself as Dave Bennet, London cabby. "How the fuck am I going to get new trucks in this shit hole?" he asked rhetorically.

"Tea?" said the Driver.

"Proper tea, I am pissed off with this crap they call coffee in this country! I'd love a proper brew."

The cabby followed the Driver back to his make shift camp where he unpacked his teabags and made them a cup. "Bloody marvellous," said the cabby as he took a sip.

"So, tell me what's a London taxi driver doing out here?"

"Simple really, the wife and I were watching the telly one night and they showed the poor buggers in Aleppo. The kids starving and all that shit, so I started shooting my big gob off, as usual, saying how somebody ought to do something to help. I was giving it large about how no bastard ever gets off their fat arse and does anything and then she says to me that perhaps I should get off my fat arse and do something if I felt that strongly about it. So I fucking did. I got an appeal going. Got the London Taxi Drivers association involved and Bob's your uncle, I find myself here, in the armpits of the World completely fucked."

"Seemed a good idea at the time I suppose?" said the Driver.

The cabby laughed, "Nice to hear a bit of good old British

sarcasm."

The Driver pursued the matter. "Do you have some sort of documentation for this convoy of yours or did you just turn up?"

"Of course I do. I am not a complete idiot, just a bit fucking stupid to get involved in this fuckup in the first place. I got letters from the Foreign Office, letters of passage from the UN, letters from the Turkish Consulate and I am pretty sure I have a letter from Father fucking Christmas somewhere. Every man and his dog has papers here, but the arseholes at the crossing are only interested in one thing, money. If you can pay enough you jump the queue, otherwise you can sit here with your thumb up your jacksie till the cows come home."

The Driver asked for a look at the paper work. It was all-in order and a plan formed. "I have space for your load and could move it and I have the money to pay the border guards, what I don't have is the right paperwork. Perhaps we could help one another?"

"What have you got on your wagons?" the cabby asked.

The Driver knew thee was no point in lying that he had some sort of humanitarian aid, as it would be pretty self evident what his load was when he re-branded it with the red cross paraphernalia from the cabbies' convoy," Missile launchers."

"Missile launchers, you are fucking joking. I am trying to help the poor buggers not fucking blow them up."

"I understand that and I applaud it, but as you like to say. You are fucked without me."

There was a long silence while the cabby absorbed the offer and the situation he was in. He was clearly far from happy. "I have no bleeding choice do I? Fuck, I will do what I have to do."

It was surprising how easily the bags of rice, flour and bundles of clothes and blankets could be packed around the missile launchers. The transformation was completed with buckets of white, red and blue paint that one of the soldiers brought back after a taxi ride and a trip to a supermarket.

They stood back from their handy work. They had transformed an army convoy carrying weapons into a UN Red Cross humanitarian aid hybrid within two days. The next part was the gamble that had to be taken.

Dave and the Driver gathered their paper work and took a cab to the border post along with Jazz acting as translator.

It took nearly four hours but they eventually had an audience with the post commander. "How can I help?" He looked less like anyone willing to help than the Driver had met in a long time. He did however speak English, yet another Turk who had worked in England, this time for his uncle in his Kebab restaurant in Wood Green in North London.

"We should like to cross the border, we have a humanitarian aid convoy headed for Aleppo."

"I would like to help but things are difficult and confused at the moment, the coup etcetera. I am sure matters will sort themselves in good time. You will need to be patient. Now if there is nothing else?"

The Driver slid a large packet across the table. "These are our documents. I was wondering if they would give us an exemption, they require us to have priority?"

The Captain of the guard looked into the envelope. Then he turned his back on the three of them by swivelling his chair round. He was clearly counting. That was a good sign for the Driver. It established the principle he was open to bribes and now it was just a matter of how much.

He slid the envelope back across the desk." I am not sure that your documents are completely in order, so I fear at this stage you will have to wait."

The Driver reached into his pocket and placed another envelope on top of the one sitting on the desk. "Oh! I seem to have not included these."

The Guard looked in the additional packet and picked both envelopes up and put them into his tunic inside pocket. "My men will take you to the rest stop and escort you across the border. Are you ready to go now?"

"More than ready," said the Driver, "And thank you."

Chapter 19

It was as if the day was smiling down on them as they crossed the border from Turkey into Syria. There was no wind and the sky had a large, red streak that merged into yellow and orange surrounded by a beautiful rich lilac. The colours of a Rio carnival, the Driver felt elated. How his fortunes had changed in such a short while. From being trapped in the docks in Istanbul, to being very rich was a vindication of him taking the biggest gamble of his life.

The mood amongst Jazz, his son and the other soldiers was also one of elation. They, ironically, were possibly the only refugees fleeing into Syria, the rest of the Country, was trying to go west. The Driver had given them ten thousand dollars each to drive the convoy and they hoped to make their way west and claim asylum avoiding Turkey.

Even the Taxi driver was buoyant, fulfilling his ambition to make a difference in the World. The Driver had chipped in enough money to his cause, to hire some trucks to take his aid onwards and allow the cabbie to fly back to the UK from Turkey in style.

The conversation with Adnan had been brief, now the Driver was waiting some forty kilometres inside Syria for Adnan, and most importantly, from the Driver's point of view, for the money to turn up.

The wait was not long. Adnan and Nizar had not been optimistic that their goods would make it across the border, having lost their contact in Turkey, when Mehmet was murdered, but they and the twenty or so ISIS fighters and drivers had made their way to the border just on the off chance. The coup d'etat attempt had muddied the waters and played into their hands. They had set off immediately to collect their bounty when the Driver contacted them.

The Driver could see the open backed Toyota trucks approaching and the well armed men sitting in the backs. He felt a sense of relief. In a very short time he would have his money, pay back Lesta, his dodgy Baltic Bank and get the Russian mafia off his case. He felt the excitement rise as the trucks stopped and he saw Adnan step from the cab of the first one.

"You did it," said Adnan shaking the Driver's hand.

"No thanks to you."

"What can I say? I was not to know that our contact would go and get himself murdered in a bath house."

"No, but you could have told me that you did not have the transit and export papers before I did the fucking deal."

"That is true but then you would have pulled out of the deal. We would not have our missile launcher and you would not have made a fortune. So, as they say, all's well that ends well."

The Driver did not exactly adhere to that sentiment, for he knew at this precise moment had things not gone well, he would now by running from a bunch of crazy Russian fuckers looking for their one hundred and seventy five million dollars back.

They stood quietly as Adnan's men made the rounds of the convoy and inspected the cargo on board. They were clearly pleased. They failed, however, to notice the Russian drone flying silently some forty thousand feet above, that was watching their every move.

"Satisfactory?" asked the Driver, as he handed the tablet to Adnan.

"Very, I shall make the money transfer then we shall be on our way."

The Driver waited impatiently for the payment to be transferred in to his account, "Problems?" he asked.

"Trouble with connections"

"You had better not be fucking me over," said the Driver.

"Look for yourself," he handed the tablet back to the Diver.

That was what the drone operator had been waiting for. Seeing Adnan handing back the tablet to the Driver, the operator assumed that the transaction was complete. He spoke into his headset, "mission green, go go go."

Lesta had no choice but to give up the Buks to the State for destruction, but he had managed to persuade them to, at least, allow the money to be transferred from ISIS to the Driver before wiping them from the face of the Earth. The convoy had been spotted waiting at the border and its every move had been tracked by the Russians.

The Driver and Adnan both jumped as the three Russian jets appeared roaring in the sky above them. They both dived to the ground as the planes unleashed their missiles. The heat of the explosions was unbearable and over in an instant

The stood up shaken and disorientated and looked at the trucks. They were no more, just a burning pile of twisted metal. The pilots knew their job and had done it well. Adnan, more used to air attack than the Driver, recovered his wits first. He turned and ran back to his men and their waiting vehicles.

"What about my money?" the Driver called after Adnan, but he knew the answer. He had been that close. A dodgy internet connection had cost him everything.

To his surprise his phone rang. "Please transfer our money we are waiting," Lesta said.

He was stunned. It dawned on him that he had been under surveillance from a drone or satellite. "I don't have it."

"Don't fuck with me. You were observed receiving payment. I have just received confirmation from the drone operator. Make the transfer."

"I can't," he said lamely.

"You are a dead man," and the phone went silent.

Chapter 20

Vasiliev Nikhil, Sokolov Yerik and Volkov Lesta the ultimate beneficiaries of the Baltic Bank sat round the television in Nikhil's Moscow apartment. On the screen was a bird's eye view of the Turkish Syrian border. The images from the drone were as good a quality as you would experience at the movies. The men lent forward as the Convoy came into sharp focus.

The camera zoomed in to the exchange between Adnan and the Driver.

"There, he hands him the computer and you can clearly see the Arab tapping away at the key board," said Lesta.

"I agree he is definitely making the transfer. Look here is where he hands it back," said Nikhil.

The air strike began and ended with the destruction of the convoy. All three were impressed with the precision of the missile attack. The drone remained in place long enough to capture the aftermath and confirm that the shipment had been complexly destroyed.

"Look, you can just see the fucker answering his phone to me," said Lesta. As the drone flew from the scene of carnage, the Driver could clearly be seen at the edge of the shot pulling his mobile out and putting it to his ear.

"There is no doubt that he was paid before the Buks were destroyed."

"Find him and either get the one point seven five million or kill the fuck. We have to send a message, or every piece of shit we lend money to, or launder money for, will think they can take the piss," said Nikhil.

"We will, I assure you, make a fucking example of him, trust me."

"Now look at this," said Yerik.

After a pause the screen sprang to life again as Yerik pressed buttons on the remote. The BBC news from England appeared on the screen. The headline was a leaked report on the investigation of the shooting down of a passenger jet over the Ukraine. The news reader announced that the report confirmed the jet had been downed by Russian Buks and showed footage of the launcher being moved around on a lorry.

"That does, sort of, look like our launchers being driven across the border from Russia into the Ukraine. Doesn't it?"

"Watch"

The clip cut to an interview on the late night programme "News Night", again on the BBC. The Russian spokesman was being questioned by the interviewer as to Russia's involvement.

"We totally deny any involvement and state that no Russian missiles were deployed against civilian aircraft. There were many military groups operating in the area and in the confusion of war, these things happen, but I stress that there were no Russian involvement." Yerik switched off the television with his remote.

"The Kremlin is satisfied that any link was destroyed and waited until the money was transferred before they ordered the air strike. We just have to find the fucker with our money and either get our money back or kill him," said Lesta

"Or both," said Nikhil, as they all laughed.

At that point in time, the object of the Russian's search and kill mission was in central London using a phone box.

"I need help, you have to help me or I am dead," the Driver said into the receiver.

The voice at the end of the phone sounded disappointed and resigned in equal measures. "Again when will this stop?"

"Please, I am desperate. I owe nearly two hundred million to a group of Russians."

"Are you insane, who are they?"

"They run a bank that launders money for the Russian mafia, drug dealers, everybody. It is big bucks and they don't fuck about. You pay or you die."

There was a silence. "Give me their names?"

He did and he was given a place to pick up a key and an address. "Thank you" he said as he hung up.

Several hours later he sat in the small flat in Dartford, a small town about twenty miles south of London. The flat was in what had been a Church before conversion. He looked at the stained glass window that had been dissected by the floor that had been built to give and upper and lower level. The flat contained the upper part of the window that was arched and depicted the upper torso and halo over the head of a Saint. The rest of the tableau was lost in the lower portion so there was no way of identifying the Saint in question. He sat just staring at the light filtering in, wondering what he could do now.

He was without funds. Any attempt to access his bank accounts would lead them to him as would use of the internet. His credit cards were useless, he had bought an unregistered pay as you go phone as his means of communication. He knew that if he was to survive and not be tracked down and killed, he had to live completely off the radar, buy everything with cash, not drive for fear of being stopped and having his license run through a computer check, not work or use his passport. In short, if he wanted to live, he had to live as a non-existent dead man.

He knew in the end he would be found, these people would never give up. They had the resources and they would never let anyone get away with stealing from them. To do so would be to invite every criminal to do the same. They could show no weakness.

He was a hunted animal and he had only one friend he could rely on. Only one person he could always trust. For now he had a roof and sustenance and one small glimmer of hope that the person he had known all his life would help somehow.

Chapter 21

Hambros Benedict was not in the best of humour has he stood on his terrace and looked out across the marina in Monaco. He had been trying to contact the Driver for days, but had heard nothing. He had taken him from nowhere to massive wealth. He had passed the business to him and now it seems he had been repaid by the theft of his twenty five million dollars.

He went inside as Mimi looked up from her laptop. "I found two gorgeous guys on the net who are vacationing in Monte Carlo." He moved across to view the screen. The two men going under the names randyjim6552 and tomcock85 did look well endowed and obviously both worked out regularly, as evidenced by their muscled frames.

"Can I fuck them, please?" she said in a silly schoolgirl voice.

"Why not, I could do with a bit of distraction and fornication."

"I am glad you said that, I invited them over this afternoon."

As the time approached for their arrival he could see his wife becoming increasing agitated as the sexual tension increased. He took a Viagra and undressed, apart from a dressing gown. She was in the bedroom when the entry phone buzzed. Mimi left the bedroom completely naked and crossed the lounge to the hallway where she pressed the enter button.

The sight of his wife, sexually aroused, had the same effect on him as his penis became erect. She entered naked holding the penis of one of the guests, which she had pulled from his trousers immediately on their entry into the flat. Benedict thought she was obviously very keen, which was not unusual. There was hardly a word spoken as she led the men to the centre of the lounge. She began to suck the now erect cock that she had led into the room. He was big, but she was undaunted. She had overcome her gag reflex years before working as a prostate in the Philippines.

The second man began to undress and showed he was even better endowed as he stroked his erect penis. When he was completely naked, Mimi turned her attention to his hard penis giving him a blow job, while the other participant rid himself of all his clothing.

Benedict was enjoying the sight of his young wife 'sucking cock' and undoing his dressing gown began to slowly stoke his penis. His wife assumed a doggy position and while one fucked her from behind she sucked the cock s of the other.

The pace quickened as the three fucked and groaned ever louder. Benedict, while rubbing his penis furiously became increasingly aroused at the prospect of his wife being filled with semen, which he would clean from her orifices with his tongue, before ejaculating in the process.

Mimi was in the throes of sexual ecstasy, "Fuck me in the arse, fuck me," she wailed, completely lost in her orgasmic arousal. He retracted his penis from her cunt and slowly entered her anus. "Yes, yes, harder, fuck my arse."

The intensity became too much and the sodomising male tensed and groaned loudly as he came in her arsehole. Benedict nearly came, but managed to control himself. He wanted to just lick the cum from her. He needed to wait until the second man had discharged his load into her mouth before he moved in to kiss and lick her.

The first man, having filled her arse with semen bent down and rummaged in the pile of clothes he had discarded. Benedict was unclear what was happening, or how it happened, but almost instantly there was a knife to Mimi's throat. The scene was frozen. Her mouth was still latched onto the other's cock. Her head was pulled back by her hair and the knife was pressed against the side of her neck. The knife was professional black, serrated and diamond sharp, a hunters or a killer's knife.

The sight of the knife stopped Benedict's masturbation immediately. He froze, one hand holding his now flaccid penis. The sight of the knife had the opposite effect on the individual Mimi was sucking off. He fucked her mouth vigorously and ejaculated. The semen dribbled from the side of her mouth, as he withdrew his penis.

He walked over to Benedict, his penis still semi erect, dripping saliva and the remains of the ejaculate. He now realised, as the man approached, how toned and muscled he actually was. He also saw the total lack of emotion in the man. Too late he realised that these two men were not the usual fuck partners that entertained him and his wife. They were trained killers, probably ex Special Forces in someone's army.

"Where is the Driver?" The accent clearly betrayed whose army's Special Forces, the Russians.

"I don't know, please don't hurt my wife," he pleaded, his eyes fixed on the knife at the neck and his sperm covered wife.

"Your slut wife will not be with you much longer if you don't tell us where to find the piece of shit who owes the money to my bosses."

The silence seemed to last for hours as Benedict sat there looking at Lesta's and the Baltic banks official debt recovery agents. He had no answers. He wanted his money as well, but it was clear that the Driver had not only vanished with his, but also the Russians money. "Please," he said.

Randyjim6552 just stared at him unmoving. "I ask you one last time. Where is the Driver?"

"I don't know."

He moved his hand in signal to Tomcock85 and Mimi screamed. The knife was drawn across her throat and the scream subsided into a gurgle and a choke before silence, apart from the sound of Benedict's own wail of anguish. He tried to rise from his chair, but the retraining arms were too powerful. The knife was used in a sawing action to completely sever the head. The naked man carrying the head dripping in blood and semen, deposited it in Benedict's lap onto his now shrivelled penis.

Randyjim6552 took the knife from Mimi's killer and held it to Benedict's neck. Tomcock85 made his way to the bathroom to shower and wash Mimi's blood from his body.

"We will be back, you have a week to find the Driver, or you had better find some where to run and hide where we can't find you."

Both dressed, they left the apartment. Hambros Benedict was completely in shock. He knew that the police would be unable to trace the DNA of these men. They would match it to previous murders, but they would never be able to apprehend them and they would never be extradited from Russia, or they would claim diplomatic immunity. No amount of evidence would make any difference. The Russians always harboured their own.

In any case, these men, were just tools, the real culprit was the Driver. Benedict now felt such hatred to this man he had treated as a son, that he would gladly have handed him over to anyone capable of torturing and killing him.

Chapter 22

"I do," said Tim.

"I now pronounce you man and wife," said the Registrar.

Tim kissed Jackie and the guests all applauded. They sat beaming as they signed the Register, the photographer took countless shots until he was happy with the results.

"That was close," said Tim. "Stiles forgot the button holes and in the end we ended up having to run here from the car park. I only just beat you through the door."

"Well, was it worth the running?" Jackie asked.

"I'll find out tonight."

"You might not, if you are not nice to my Mum."

The guest lined up and despite the official warning about the throwing of confetti, they were picking bits off each other as they sat in the back of the wedding car heading to the reception.

Tim had no parents or siblings and Jackie was also an only child, so the reception line just consisted of the two of them and Jackie's parents. "Mr Routledge, I wonder if you could do me a favour while I think of it?" said Tim.

"Call me Dad" he said. "Just joking you can call me Sir," he laughed.

"The postman was trying to deliver a packet that needed signing for when we dashed out. Would you pick it up from the sorting office while we are away, so they don't return it to the sender for non-collection?"

"Will do"

Stiles' speech as best man was less than complementary, but better than most. Her Father welcomed him formally to the family. Daniel, Jackie's son, a boy of ten gave him a big hug, it really touched him being called him Dad, before being sick, having eaten too many sweets that were in bowls on the guest tables. He recovered soon enough and was demonstrating his dancing ability when the DJ started the music.

Jackie and Tim did mingling and wedding present thanking duties before opening the dancing with the first waltz, or more accurately, in Tim's case, a sort of zombie shuffle.

"Lovely wedding" said Elaine, "This is my son Nicky."

Shaking his hand, Tim asked "Was your husband not well enough to come?"

"No, I am afraid he will only get steadily worse."

"I am so sorry," said Jackie.

"Please don't be, we have had a good life together and I have a lovely son," she ruffled his hair playfully despite the fact that Nicky was in his thirties. It lightened the awkwardness that falls on any discussion centred on terminal illness.

Cake cut, bouquet tossed and goodbyes said they settled back for the drive to the airport hotel. Jackie pulled her shoes off. "That's better. I really don't know how Elaine can walk in the shoes she had on?"

Tim laughed, "She does like her shoes. To be fair to Elaine the ones she had on today would be considered sensible, compared to the usual footwear she has in the office. She has about twenty pairs of designer shoes in the bottom of her office cabinet, just in case."

"Just in case of what?"

"Not sure really, just in case she needs a pair that she can't walk in I suppose."

The car pulled up at the hotel and the Driver opened the door for them. While he collected the luggage from the boot, they made their way to the desk. The girl behind the counter cocked her head and waited.

"I'll do it," said Jackie.

"Room for Mr and Mrs Burr" she said with a giggle. The girl looked somewhat puzzled at the enthusiastic way Jackie and announced themselves.

"Just married today," said Tim by way of explanation.

"Right," said the girl, totally disinterested and in a monotone continued. "Room eighteen, lifts are to the left, do you want breakfast?" She handed them the plastic key.

"Cheery soul," said Jackie as they struggled into their room with the luggage.

"Well not everyone can appreciate how wonderful I am," said Tim "and I think I was very nice to your Mum and Dad, don't you?"

"You were and you will get your reward, just let me give Daniel a ring to say good night and then you can fuck me stupid."

"Sounds like a plan." He took her in his arms and kissed her slowly. "I do love you so much," he said.

They awoke, tired with a lack of sleep and took a taxi to the airport. "Next, the wonders of ancient Egypt and the Nile," he said as their checked in their luggage.

Chapter 23

Randyjim6552 and tomcock85 bordered the Lady Heloise in Monte Carlo's marina. The luxury yacht owned by Sokolov Yerik was an eye turner, even for the boating elite in Monaco. The sea was clear, calm and the crisp, cool morning air intensified the blue, of the waters along the Cote D'Azure. She was bound for Alexander in Egypt where Yerik was due to join her on board. Randyjim6552 and tomcock85 were just part of the group of ex Special Forces thugs that Yerik had on board, as well as the actual seamen and allied staff, comprising cleaners, cooks and maids. In effect the yacht was a floating luxury hotel that could be hired out for thousands of dollars a day, or was ready as a base for Yerik anywhere, she was needed.

The Lady Heloise was needed off the coast of Egypt to welcome a prisoner on board. Events had moved quickly over the last few days for the three Russian oligarchs and their money laundering Baltic Bank and not for the good. Jackie Burr's friend and Finance Director of the Baltic Bank, had come into possession of documents revealing the true owners of the operation. The papers proved categorically that the assets of the bank were, ultimately, owned by the rich and not so good Russian elite.

Tensions had begun between the Americans and the Russians over the Crimea and the recent escalation in Syria of Russian support for the Assad regime had intensifies the tension between the two Countries. The US were out to cause as much economic damage as they could. If the CIA came into possession of the documents, they would have the ability to track down and seize the wealth of some of the most prominent citizens of that Country.

Yerik, Nikhil and Lesta would overnight become the least popular men on the Planet, with the Russians and, consequently, their time left on the Planet would in turn be very short lived.

Yerik could hardly believe how things had gone from bad to worse, to even worse in such a short period of time. First, the Driver had stolen over a hundred and seventy five million from them. Then incrementing paper work, with their true names plastered all over, it had been stolen and sent to some auditor woman in England. They had tracked her down and found she had been married and was on honeymoon in Egypt. To make matters worse, her husband worked for British intelligence. They had burgled their home in the hope of finding the papers, but had found nothing.

He marvelled at the extent of the ability of his, so called, highly trained security staff, to compound a fuck up, by even greater fuck ups. In a desperate attempt to recover the papers he had sent his best man to London to abduct this woman's son, Daniel, in an attempt to force her to return the file. That had been, an almighty balls up, resulting in his men being shot on the streets of London by an armed response unit. They failed to abduct the boy, shot the Grandparents, at whose house he was staying, while his Mother was on honeymoon and got themselves killed in the process.

Yerik knew he had one last roll of the dice. He had sent a team to Egypt to abduct this bloody woman and force her to reveal where she had the documents housed. He knew that she was the accountant in charge of the audit, a role her friend the Finance Director of the Baltic bank, Maurice Lee, had secured for her. He knew she did not have time to take the papers to the offices of the Accountancy Practice, because they would have either arrived on the day before, or the day of her wedding.

As Yerik packed in readiness of his flight to Cairo and subsequent transfer to the Lady Heloise, Tim and Jackie had just received the terrible news that her Parents had been attacked in a home invasion. Their Nile cruise boat was moored in Luxor and arrangements had been hastily made to fly them back to the UK

"I'll make my way to the taxi," Jackie called to Tim, who was dealing with a few last minutes details aboard the boat with George, who had been so helpful to them when the news had reached them. She just wanted to get back home to her son, Daniel and to see her Mum and Dad in hospital. She walked slowly up the gangplank, distracted by her thoughts and failed to notice Yerik's men as they walked towards her. Tim was still in conversation with George and was, also, distracted.

The next few seconds were a blur. She was aware of the men appearing, being half carried and half dragged to a waiting car. The fear brought on a rush of adrenaline, things seemed to move in slow motion as her heightened senses, caused by the fear response, recorded every minute detail of the events.

She opened her mouth to scream but a hand was placed firmly across it covering both her mouth and nose. She feared she was suffocating as she was hauled into the car. There were a number of passer-by's and drivers of the horse drawn carriages that plied their trade along the mooring site of all the Nile cruisers, but despite her desperate struggling, not a single one made any attempt to help her. They were indifferent to the plight of a woman. Their cultural norm had conditioned them to the extent that it was acceptable for an errant woman to be restrained or disciplined by her husband. They were certainly not involving themselves in the plight of a brazen western woman, so the kidnappers acted without any danger of intervention.

She bit the hand that was covering her mouth and screamed as it was withdrawn. The crowd merely watched. She saw Tim react and give chase, then the black of unconsciousness as she was punched and driven off.

Chapter 24

"Listen to this," said Jeff Stiles, deputy head of MI5. He was sat in Elaine Wilkins' office in Thames House, MI5 Headquarters. Tim had returned from Luxor several days ago and the Service had devoted a great deal of its resources to establishing the facts behind his wife's abduction and the attack on her family. The fact that there were two dead Russians, killed following the home invasion of his parents in-law, who both were known to work for a well known Russian oligarch called Sokolov Yerik, made life a lot easier in putting them on the right track.

They had asked and received help from agencies around the globe in tracking Yerik's movements. It was easily established that he was on his luxury, billion dollar yacht, the Lady Heloise, bobbing around the Med. The fact that his henchmen had tried to abduct Jackie's son in London and that now she had been taken in Egypt convinced them that she was being held on the Yacht.

"What is it?" asked Elaine.

"A recording of a phone call Tim has just had from his wife."

He pressed the play button and they sat in silence as the conversation played out. They were watching and monitoring Tim's every move and conversation. Elaine had decided that they would make all efforts in the protection of one of their own. She was treating this as a direct attack on MI5. She realised that Tim would be in a highly emotional state and his judgment would be impaired. So he was closely watched for his own sake. She did not want a further tragedy on her hands, owing to Tim's closeness to the situation.

"Tim is that you?"

"Jackie, are you alright?" Tim's concern was plain to hear in his voice, a mixture of relief and fear for her wellbeing.

"I'm fine. Is Daniel safe and my Mum and Dad?"

"They are safe and protected at all times. No one will get to them now. Your Mum has been shot but she is on the mend."

"What about Dad, tell me?"

"He is alive, but suffered a stroke. I am sorry, it is a case of wait and see, but he is in no imminent danger."

Jackie could be heard taking a deep intake of breath and stifling back sobs. "Don't worry," said Tim, "it will be ok. I know what they want."

A male voice heavily accented came on the line. "Mr Burr, you need to listen carefully."

"Mr Yerik..." Tim interrupted.

"You know who I am?"

"I have your file and its gives me not only your details, but the details of all the other scumbags who are involved as well. It didn't take a genius to link the dead pieces of shit we shot in London back to you. You should also know that MI6 and the Navy are also tracking your boat as you fuck about in the Med. If anything happens to my wife they will blow your tiny boat out of the water and say you were a human trafficker smuggling people from Libya. So be very careful what you say next."

There was a silence. Yerik was clearly shaken by what he had heard. "I see," he said slowly. "You obviously have the file that links my friends and me to our banking operation."

"I have the file. You couldn't find it when you burgled our home because it was in the boot of my Father in law's car. He had picked it up from the Post Office sorting office while we were on honeymoon. He had forgotten all about it."

"What have you done with it Mr Burr?"

"It is safe. If anything happens to me it will be sent to the Americans, they will have a field day seizing all your assets Worldwide and the assets of all your cronies. I don't give much hope of your living to a ripe old age when they find out you were the arsehole that lost them their grubby fortunes. Do you?"

"I think your analysis of my predicament is totally accurate and I might add I would appreciate if you didn't get yourself killed before we can make a trade. You are going to trade are you not?"

"My wife for the original documentation, where and when?" said Tim

"I will text the GPS coordinates and the time. Say goodbye to your wife."

Jackie came on the phone. "Be careful, I love you."

"Don't worry, it'll be fine. Love you too."

The phone went silent. Stiles handed the coordinates to Elaine., "Crete by Souda Bay."

"Where is Tim now? She asked.

"He is being held in an interview room in the basement. After he received the phone call he went to a depository where he had hidden the file. I had him picked up and brought back here. He had his passport and e-ticket for Crete on him." Stiles pushed the file across the table to Elaine.

She studied the file for a few moments. "The CIA would kill for this. It is proof, positive of the ownership of all the loot these Russians have stashed outside of Russia. They could really ramp up the pressure on the Kremlin if they seized this lot."

"We need to hand it to MI6 or the Foreign Office so they can give it to the Yanks."

"That would condemn Tim's wife to death," she said.

"What choice is there? He is my friend but we are talking about the security of this Country."

Elaine was silent and looked down at her latest pair of badly fitting, but beautifully designed shoes. "You and I know nothing will really be done with this file. It wouldn't be made public, it would be used around the negotiating table to put pressure on the Russians to, for example, cut back on bombing the anti-Assad forces in Syria, or negotiate a few concessions in the Ukraine. Ultimately it would do very little in the whole scheme of things."

Stiles was silent. It was a very big call. Save his friend and his wife or score a few points off the Kremlin. "What file, I never saw it."

"Neither did I" said Elaine.

"How do we proceed?"

"In for a penny, in for a pound as they say, we give it the works. First get onto the Home office and get Diplomatic passports for Tim and Jackie, not in their own names."

Stiles interrupted, "I shall go with him as back up."

There was a pause as she considered it. "Ok, get three CD passports, get guns, flak jackets, money and whatever else you think you will need. Stick the lot in the diplomatic pouch, which will be the size of a trunk, so you avoid customs and security

112

inspections and book flights and accommodation."

"We will need help. Yerik will not just let us walk away. We could still give testimony first hand linking them to the file, even if we only have a copy and not the original. A copy of the file with Tim's and my sworn deposition saying that we passed it to him, would still put the Russians in a tight spot. Killing the three of us would be his best strategy once he has the original in his hands."

"Leave that to me. You will have more back up than you could hope for and with a bit of luck we will retain the files and be heroes with the CIA and MI6."

Stiles left and Elaine pulled strings. By the time Tim and Stiles were on their way to Crete. There was a Destroyer diverted from it's role off the coast of Libya, where it had been stationed to interrupt the activities of the immigrant smugglers from Africa to Europe and a squad of Special Forces, ready to be deployed at the rendezvous point where Jackie and the files were to be traded.

Chapter 25

Jackie was brought up on deck. The whirling of the helicopter blades added to the chill of the night air as she was herded across the helipad. The moon was a bright ball in sky, whose reflected light lit up the water and cliffs surrounding Souda Bay on the island of Crete. Yerik was sat in the front alongside the pilot and she in the back with the powerfully built henchman that shadowed Yerik's every footstep.

The pilot flew directly upwards before tilting the helicopter nose down at full speed, heading directly north towards the hills behind the bay. It was the first time that Jackie had been in a helicopter, but this was no joy ride and enjoyment was certainly not part of the experience. All she wanted was to be back at home seeing her son Daniel and her Parents. She was feeling hope that the ordeal would soon be over and dread that this could end tragically and she would never see her family again.

The helicopter approached the rendezvous point. She could make out the two cars below with their headlights on. The four figures, two stood by each vehicle were, at first, mere silhouettes in the moonlight, but as the aircraft descended, the individuals became identifiable. There were Yerik's two goons, randyjim6552 and tomcock85 whom she knew from the yacht and then her heart lifted as she recognised Stiles and her husband waiting below.

The helicopter did not immediately descend, but switched on a powerful searchlight and hovered above the ground. It flew above the meeting point, searching for any concealed individuals who may have been posted to intercept them. Yerik, the pilot and his guard were all staring intently at the barren plateau, looking for signs of life. All Jackie could see was the odd bit of scrub, boulders and limestone screed. It all appeared clear and deserted. That was not so. Had the craft been equipped with a heat seeking camera, the squad of Special Services personnel would have shown up a bright red on the screen. As it was, they remained totally concealed from the observers, metres from where the helicopter landed, almost within touching distance of the protagonists on the plateau.

The next few moments were all a blur. The sequence of events, that ensued were too rapid for her brain to process. She was forced, to step from the helicopter. There was an exchange of words between her husband and Yerik. Stiles stepped forward with the file she had been sent by her friend and Finance Director of the Baltic Bank. A file that she had never seen or knew existed, the file that had caused the shooting of her Parents, the attempted abduction of her son and her own abduction and imprisonment.

The trade was made and she was with her husband when the shooting began. She saw Stiles, hit by a bullet, fall. Then the whole area was suddenly filled with men that seemed to appear from the ground, as the Special Boat Service joined the fray. Yerik and his goons surrendered immediately to the overwhelming fire power. A Navel helicopter, attached to the Destroyer anchored in the bay, had appeared overhead, Yerik, his goons, vehicle and helicopter were all sent packing.

She was surprised to see Stiles miraculously recover, before she realised he had been wearing a bullet proof vest. She kissed and held Tim as they drove off from the plateau with the file still in their possession. The nightmare was over and she was relieved when they arrived back at the Golf resort Hotel where Tim and Stiles had booked in. The relief and happiness was further enhanced when she had spoken to her son and Mother on the phone.

Reunited with her husband, the lovemaking had been intense and passionate for the newlyweds. They fell into a content and relaxed sleep.

The next morning they had awoken too late to have breakfast and Tim had gone off to buy provisions when Stiles knocked on the door.

"Come in" she said. "I am making coffee. They provide a filter machine, coffee and long life milk. Not great but it will have to do."

He entered the apartment and noticed that the file containing the proof of the Oligarch's involvement in the banking scams was lying on the dining table. Yerik was miles out at sea being watched by the Navy. He no longer posed a threat.

Stiles noticed that the apartment was identical to his. You entered, the dining table was to your right, the kitchen, effectively in the corridor, to your left, leading to the bathroom and bedroom and directly ahead, a seating area with a French window to the ground level terrace.

"Go out to the terrace, I'll bring the coffee out," she said, as he passed her in the kitchen area.

The terrace had a table and four chairs and several cats waiting to see if any food would appear. A low metal fence separated the paved terrace from the landscaped gardens beyond. Stiles noted that stepping over the fence and crossing the garden would be a quicker route to the car park than leaving via the door and walking around the Complex and following the paths.

He sat down in one of the chairs and looked out across to the distant hills. The Golf Resort Hotel complex was built atop a hill itself and afforded beautiful views over the rugged Cretan countryside. The distant hills were covered in a mist and some, he could see were snow capped. Where they were located, the weather was warm and mild with the sun nearly overhead, while in contrast the tips of the mountains were close to freezing.

"Here's the coffee, if you can call it that," said Jackie as she came through the French doors and sat down beside him. He picked up his cup and took a sip and grimaced.

"Perfect, thank you," he lied.

"I feel like we are on holiday," she took a sip of her coffee.

"Well it is all over now, you can relax. How do you feel?"

She paused as she tried to clarify her thoughts." Mostly confused, none of it really makes sense. I was on honeymoon having the time of my life. Then I learn my Parents have been shot and before I can come to terms with that, I am abducted. Then I learn that one of my oldest friends, Maurice, who I qualified with and who helped my career by getting me the audit of the Baltic Bank he worked at, is dead, murdered for sending me some papers exposing my new audit as a scam front for Russian organised crime.."

"Those papers establish ownership of billions of dollars squirreled by the crooked elite in Russia. Just the sort of dodgy money the Americans want to seize to put pressure on the Kremlin. You're safe and the evidence is on the dining table. The bastards who orchestrated this assault on you and your family will get what's coming to them when we hand the file to the Yanks," said Stiles.

They sat back and waited for Tim to come back with their brunch. Jackie closed her eyes and let the sun warm her face. She could hear the sound of crickets chirping and the rustle of foliage as the numerous stray cats stalked their way through the undergrowth and shrub surrounding the terrace, looking for a meal. Most of the cats had wondered off, realising that there was no food to be had on the terrace.

The horror of the last few days faded into the background as she soaked up the late season sun in the tranquil surroundings. She started when Stiles' voice interrupted her daydreaming.

"You," was the only word he uttered before the bullet fired from the silenced gun entered his brain.

She did not have time to open her eyes, before she too died with a shot to her head.

The Driver stepped over the low metal fence and walked past the two dead bodies and began to search. Within a minute, he saw the file just sitting in the middle of the dining table. Hardly believing the ease in which he had located his prize, he walked back out of the French windows to the car park.

Tim would return and find their bodies surrounded by the stray cats lapping up the blood that had pooled on the terrace.

Chapter 26

Elaine looked down at her shoes. They suddenly seemed less important than they were a few weeks earlier. The funerals of Jackie and Stiles had left her no longer the confident strong person she had felt herself to be. An attack on MI5 had taken place and while everyone knew that the Russians were behind it, nothing was to be done. In the good old days of the cold war, MI6 would have sent a man with a gun to seek revenge and let it be known that the UK and the US stood firm against the Soviet Union. Now the US was more or less moribund in their relations with the Russians. Despite a lot of table banging, Putin had continued the bombing campaign in Syria, supporting Assad and NATO and the Americans had done nothing.

The Russians were emboldened, following the invasion of the Crimea, with no response from the West. The former Soviet states were now firmly in the Russians sights, with demands already being made for NATO troops to be withdrawn from the area. The death of an MI5 operative did not weigh heavily in the scheme of things.

They had recruited Tim to fill Stiles' role as deputy head. She knew it was not an ideal choice, but the options had been limited. He was embittered by the murder of his wife and she knew that, as such, his judgement would be clouded. On the other hand, he was battle blooded, intensely focussed and obsessed with the Isis and Russian threat to the UK. It was a case of mend and make do and it might all work out for the best.

Time knocked and entered the office. She saw the dark circles under his eyes, through lack of sleep. He was following every line of inquiry personally in the hope of finding his wife's killer.

"How are you finding it?"

"Hard going, I am about two thirds of the way through Stiles' case files. I popped in to see if you could add any background to some stuff he was working on?"

"Fire away," she immediately regretted her choice of words.

"Well, one thing caught my attention. He was tracking some arms deal with Isis, headed for Syria. Looking at some dealer, Hambros Benedict, and there seemed a link to the Baltic Bank and the Russians, any thoughts?"

Elaine let out a sigh." I told him to leave it alone umpteen times. It has nothing to do with us. I told him to pass it to MI6 or the Yanks. We have enough to do here without worrying about Syria."

"But," he began to speak.

"But, you want to follow it up because it has that Bank and those Russian scumbags involved. I say to you that it still has nothing to do with what we are supposed to be doing at MI5. I say the same to you as I said to Stiles, drop it."

He looked crestfallen and she understood his need to feel he was doing all he could to track down his wife's killer. She spoke in a more conciliatory fashion. "Look, I do understand how you feel. I feel the same way, but we have to concentrate on our counter espionage roll. Diverting resources to a personal vendetta does not serve this Country well. You have to understand that?"

He nodded his understanding and made his way back to his desk. He may have understood, but he had no intention of doing anything other than tracking down his wife's murderer. He took the job for one reason alone, to use the resources available to MI5 to get the bastard.

He ran through mentally what he knew and what he could

surmise. On his desk he had the report of the Greek police investigation. He read through it. The autopsy report showing that Stiles and his wife had received one shot to the head each. Two nine millimetre bullets were recovered from them. The two bullets were matched to each other, so there had been one gun and, presumably, one shooter.

There had been no witnesses. The guests staying at the hotel complex had been checked out and none had raised suspicion or had any links to organised crime. They were holidaying couples, groups of golfers, not assassins. The Greek police had checked plane manifests and nothing unusual was noted. In short, they had generated no leads.

Tim knew the motive. The files with Yerik's, Nikhil's and Lesta's signatures plastered all over them, implicating them in a massive money laundering and assets concealment scheme for themselves and their fellow Russian mafia mates.

The opportunity, however, was proving far more problematic as none of the three were near the scene of the murder. Yerik was on the Lady Heloise, being shadowed by the Royal Navy and had clearly sailed straight back to Monaco, where the Yacht had berthed. Nikhil and Lesta, Tim knew had not been hands on in the affair and were, in any event, at a meeting in St Petersburg with half a dozen witnesses to the fact.

Some third party, logically, had to have committed the murder as the prime suspects and their thug entourage were accounted for. He speculated that they had hired a hit man, but again he come to the conclusion that it defied logic to arrange a killing of someone you could already have killed yourself. It was evident that Yerik had no intention of letting Jackie, Stiles or him live after the file had been handed over. Had the SBS not intervened, the three of them would have been killed in the hills overlooking Souda Bay.

He had to rule out a professional hit man employed by the

oligarchs, as in their plan there would be no one to kill apart from three already deceased targets. That left the harder prospect to investigate, that some one independent had killed them and taken the file. Tim considered that it must be the only explanation, but the motive now became muddied. The file was the object of the murder, but it only had value to the three Russians. What would a third party need it for? There were two possibilities, the file indicated another person, or that person wanted the file to ingratiate himself with the Russians, or perhaps apply leverage to them.

Tim pulled up a copy of the source of all the deaths, the paper work for the Baltic Bank. The file had been scanned into the system prior to Stiles and his departure for Crete. The copy was of no value, but it did act as a valuable record of the actions of the three. He read and re-read every detail, but there was no indication of any other person involved. The conclusion was clear. A third party had taken the file and killed them for the purpose of blackmailing the Russians. Tim however, realised he was no closer to identifying the killer, but at least he had the motive.

One big question jumped out and smacked Tim in the face.

"How the fuck did the killer know who they were and how did he know where to find us?" he said to himself. They had travelled under fake diplomatic passports. The hotel was booked at the last minute in fake names. They had booked and flown within hours. It was impossible, given the time span for anyone to locate them or to have followed them.

The more he thought about it, the more impossible it seemed to accomplish. "How do you get a gun through airport security?" he said aloud. Stiles and he had used the entire diplomatic immunity protocols to get their weapons to Crete. How had one man managed to do it unaided?

Tim only had one lead and that was what every crime

investigation started with, "Follow the money". He would start with the Baltic Bank and work outwards.

Chapter 27

The bar was packed, despite the snow and the bitter cold, the punters were in tonight watching the girls dancing naked on the podium. The cliental was mostly local Muscovites. The tourists and foreign businessmen preferred not to travel to the city when winter starts. Lesta and Yerik stood at the bar off to left of the podium and drank vodka, served by a young topless bartender. Despite the sight of all the naked young female flesh on display, they were less than happy.

"I am too old for all this shit. The fucking music is giving me a headache," shouted Lesta, trying to make himself heard over the hubbub.

Yerik smiled and nodded. It was clear he was unable to make out what had been said to him, so he chose just to pretend he had. The bar was one of many that Nikhil had invested in. He owned bars and clubs from Moscow to Paris and London to New York. He had been successful and in places like London, Russian mafia money controlled virtually all the night scene in the city.

"Why, the fuck, are we here," continued a less than happy Lesta. To which Yerik nodded and smiled politely in response. "Oh for fucks sake, why don't you get a fucking hearing aid?"

Lesta had enough and was on the verge of leaving, or strangling a nodding Yerik, when Nikhil entered the club. He gestured them to follow as he went past the stage to the office at the rear of the club.

Sitting in the relative quite of the office the conversation opened with Lesta. "What a fucking shit hole," he said.

"A successful shit hole though," said Nikhil. "I apologise for the location, but I have been running round Moscow all day and still have stuff to do. But we do need to talk about the fucking balls up in Crete. What I can't understand is why there has been no action from the Yanks. Surely they have the file linking us to all the money stashed overseas by now. Why haven't they frozen the money?"

"I may have the answer," said Yerik. He reached into his pocket and pulled out a sheet of paper and handed it to Nikhil, who began to read.

"What does it mean?" he asked as he passed the copy of an email to Lesta.

"It means that the reason the Americans have not come down on us like a ton of bricks, is that they do not have the file, the Driver does, or says he does." said Lesta.

"How can he have the file?"

"This may help." Yerik passed a further piece of paper across the desk to Nikhil, This time a print out of a news item. "It doesn't give much detail but the day after I was sent packing by the Navy, two people were murdered on Crete."

"And you think this has something to do with our file, how?"

"Let's suppose the deceased are the husband and wife and somehow the Driver killed them and took the file."

"He didn't know anything about the file or the woman. It is not possible. How could he find them, let alone kill them and take the file? Its bollocks," said Lesta.

"He's just trying to save his arse with a cock and bull story. Find the fuck and get him to pay up or kill him."

"What if he has the file? It is not important how he got it. We still don't want the Yanks getting it or we will be the ones with our balls cut off."

"He says to phone, so phone, either way we get closer to finding him."

The Driver was still hiding out in the flat trying to stay off the radar. He had sent the email two days earlier. He had not been idle in the mean time. On his return from Crete he had travelled to the Isle of Man and visited every crook and money launderers' favourite advocate, Graham Pelham. The lawyer was not in the least surprised to be given an envelope and issued with instructions to open it and follow the instructions contained therein, in the event the Driver failed to make contact on a monthly basis. Pelham's only interest was in the regular payment of a grand a month for the service. The Driver had ensured that if the Russians killed him, the Americans, the British and the press would be in possession of the facts and proof of the involvement of the Oligarchs in the money laundering scheme.

The phone rang, "Driver."

Lesta's voice came onto the phone, "Where is my money?"

"I never got paid because your fucking air force blew up the convoy first."

"That is your problem. Pay the fucking money or say goodbye to your cock. We will find you."

"I think you will find it has just become your problem. I have something of yours and if anything happens to me then I have ensured that you and your cronies will be shafted."

"I don't believe you."

"I thought you might say that. Are you near a computer, if so, just give me an email address?" The Driver typed in the address and pressed send.

There was a few moments pause and then the phone was put on mute. Lesta, Nikhil and Yerik looked at the scan of the last page of the document with their signatures on it as it was displayed on Nikhil's tablet.

"How, the fuck did he get that?" said Nikhil.

Lesta pressed the un-mute button on his phone. "How did you come into possession of this? How the fuck did you even know about it?"

"Does it matter? The point is I have it and I will use it to fuck you the same way you fucked me, by telling the Russian where those Buks were so they could destroy the evidence of their involvement in shooting down that passenger jet. I am not stupid. I know you fuckers had a hand in it."

Lesta interrupted him protesting his innocence

"Shut the fuck up. I wouldn't believe a word you said, even if you had the Pope as a witness, just listen. Firstly, if anything happens to me the papers will be sent to the CIA. You had better hope that I don't get run over or catch a virus, Have you got that?"

"We could tracked you down and torture their location out of you."

"It is a plan, but I am not an idiot, if I told you their location, you would kill me anyway so there would be no point, Secondly I of course need you to write off the debt."

"I worked that bit out for myself. What else," said Lesta?

"A small payment by way of recompense, say one hundred million?"

The mute button was pressed for a second time and a few

moments elapsed before Lesta came back onto the phone. "You could continually come back and ask for more, blackmailing us on and on."

"There is that, but as I said I am not stupid, I want to live out my life naturally, if I did that, sooner or later you would have moved your operation or buried it deeper or the political situation may change. Who knows, but I just want to survive this and live to old age."

"We have no choice, but be careful, I am not the forgiving type."

The Driver pressed the send button and his bank details were sent. "Make the transfer," he said into the phone and hung up.

Three minutes later the balance on the account was up by one hundred million dollars. Not the two hundred he had hoped for, but at least he lived and was rich.

The Driver had one final matter to clear up. He owed Hambros Benedict twenty five million for his part in funding the arms deal. He would phone him, pay him and remove the final danger to his health.

What he did not know was that Benedict's wife had been brutally murdered because of him. No amount of money would ever reverse that, Benedict now only lived for one thing, revenge.

Chapter 28

MI5 was coming to terms with the reality of cyber crime. The recruitment drive was beginning to produce results. The attacks by China, Russia and North Korea in the past months on the US and UK Governments, commercial and utilities such as electricity, computers was increasing. Tim was finding more and more of his time was being absorbed in dealing with the planning, strategy and placement of new technical staff.

He, however, considered all this a distraction from his prime focus of tracking down his wife's killer. He had gathered together all the information he could from every source on the three Russians and their operations. He plotted every transaction and loan he could, he had even involved the Icelandic Banking Authority, the home territory of the Baltic Bank, to aid him. They were naturally reluctant, but he played the ISIS link and terrorist threat card and they sent him all they had.

It was clear that the biggest single transaction, other than the interactions with the Icelandic Banks, were loans to Hambros Benedict and Company. It was all he had, so he ran with it. Contact with the CIA and examination of the source documentation made available to the Parliamentary Committee, looking at British arms sales to the Saudis, soon revealed that the Company was strictly minor league and had, up until recently, dealt mostly in Latin America. It was pretty evident that Benedict himself was no longer active in the industry and had moved to Monaco to retire.

Tim looked at the results from GCHQ, the UK eyes and ears on the net and telecommunications networks of the World. The problem he faced was the sheer volume of data collected.

Comprising emails, phone calls, texts, major financial transactions and targeted individual information. Wood and trees and needles in haystacks went through Tim's mind as he saw the size of the files. Banking transactions were so completely off any scale, that a human mind could not hope to analyse them. With computer algorithms, banks could execute thousands of trades in nanoseconds, which they called high frequency trading. Hundreds of millions of dollars were traded to make a few hundred on each trade. The money could be turned thousands of times in a day. The overall volume was huge, but at the end of the day, perhaps the net position could be as low as a hundred million when they balanced at the end of the day.

Tim had the man power though and he put it to work. He used the intake of new computer whiz kids to write some search algorithms to narrow the database down. He interacted so much with the technical guys that he drew praise from Elaine for his dedication in getting stuck into the threat of cyber attacks. She would not have been so impressed if she knew the amount of MI5's resources that were being diverted for his own personal quest.

"We may have something," said Harriet Shaw, one of the new breed of technical savvy recruits, who had been helping him coordinate his investigation.

She put the tablet down on his desk and turned it so he could see the screen. It meant nothing to him. The screen displayed what appeared to be a series of spiky graphs. "Tell me about it."

He gestured for her to pull a chair round to his side of the desk and sit so they could view the screen together. "This is a result of an app we wrote to search the data we had from GCHQ on banking transactions. Basically, during the referenced time frame you gave us, we looked at the probability of on a given day the Bank, or Banks, exceeding their exposure beyond their normal risk parameters."

He looked at her" Not a clue," he said.

She let out a sigh as though he was obviously a bit dim. "Look at it this way, if you are millionaire it would not be unusual to spend, say five thousand, but if you were a normal working person it would, Likewise banks need to assess risk based on their capital base. Too much exposure and if the market goes against you, you end up doing a Lehman Brothers. Now we don't know what the risk profile is for any given bank, so we cannot with any accuracy see if there is an unusual trading pattern. So we wrote a little algorithm that looks at the past trading patterns of a bank and from that we work out if a bank exceeds its limits."

"So tell me the bottom line?"

"The spikes show when the Baltic Bank pushed the envelope and then rather than rectify the position, as you would expect, it pushed it further."

"Specifically"

"Specifically tracing the spikes, Baltic lent one of the Directors' Companies, a Mr Lesta, ninety million. Then it lent another one hundred and seventy five million to an arms dealer, Hambros Benedict Limited, another then another fifty million just a week ago."

"So it made loans?" said Tim, "It is a bank after all."

"Not a very good one, it wrote the whole lot off two days after paying out the fifty million."

"Now that is what I call an unusual business transaction. Well done."

She left taking the tablet. Tim knew he was on the right track. The money and the timing fitted the events. He needed to know more about Hambros Benedict and his dealing with the Russians.

He pulled what he had, from the data, which was very little. The file started by Stiles did however, point to a new boss, running the show, known as the Driver, he had taken over from Benedict. He had a name for the Driver, James Riddle. He could find no nationality, date of birth or passport on the data bases.

"Oh bollocks," he said aloud. "James Riddle, Jimmy Riddle, fuck it." Cockney slang, to do a Jimmy was to take a piddle. Clearly he needed to delve deeper.

The current focus on cyber crime at MI5 triggered a thought. He had seen that a law firm in Panama, that had set up bogus identities to cover tax evaders, had been hacked and leading figures, dodging tax, had been ousted. He checked the eleven million documents leaked, focussing on Riddle and Hambros. The law firm had been complacent in aiding many intentional figures hide their millions and many international accountancy firms were implicated. The two were there, but were such small fry that they had attracted little or no attention. They would now.

Looking at the timing, the links from the Baltic Bank to the Russians and the link from the Bank to this Driver, Tim felt in his gut that he was onto something. He pulled up the airline passenger manifests sent to him by the Greek Police and looked for the name Riddle.

There was no hit. He felt disappointed. He and Stiles had travelled within a day to Crete and arranged their accommodation hours before their arrival. They had travelled under false names, so even had someone had access to airline bookings without knowing their names, they could not have traced them using that method. The killer must have travelled within twenty four hours to have been in position to make the hit. The only way the killer could have achieved that was by flying. No other method of getting to the Island was feasible. There was a ferry, but it went once a day and was a full day's itinerary from the mainland. He had to have flown.

He called Harriet to come back up to his office. She entered and sat down, opposite him this time.

"I need to know if you can do something. I have a list of names and passport holders and their numbers, place and date of issue. Some may be fake but most, if not all, will be genuine. I need to find the ones that are the odd ones out. Ones that spike, as you put it. I am looking in essence at what is most likely a normal passport, but is somehow not normal. I am not making sense am I?"

"You are in a funny sort of way. What you are looking for is someone who has a passport, but may have fallen outside your expectations as to how, when or where it was obtained. Further you want, in reality, to check if that person or persons have an existence beyond that passport. Were they born or have they died? Do they work? Have they had medical treatment? Have they married or had children, and so on?"

"Yes that's it. Can you do it?"

"I assume that the passports holders could be any Nationality, in that all they will have in common is that they were on a plane or planes going to a particular destination. That will make it very difficult and dependent on what information we can gather from their various Countries, where they live, were born or work."

"Concentrate on single males over thirty and under fifty."

"Easier"

"Go to it," said Tim.

Chapter 29

Hambros Benedict sat in the back of his chauffeur driven car as he was being driven from Monaco, along the Cote D'Azure to Marseilles. He was a broken man. The death of Mimi by the hands of randyjim6552 and tomcock85 had taken all that he loved and his reason for living away from. His wealth and his physical possessions now seemed to be nothing but a reminder of a former life, just garbage in a collection of lost hopes and dreams, meaningless.

The trip to the oncologist had confirmed what he knew, that time was running out. It was a matter of, perhaps weeks, and he would be joining Mimi. But he was not quite finished with the World yet. He did not intend to go alone into the after life. Others would be joining him on his journey into oblivion.

He had a list and sadness overtook him as he headed to the northern part of the city. He was sad because he knew he would be unable to take all those that deserved to die on their final journey. James Riddle, the Driver was on the list. Had he honoured his deal and paid back the Russians she would still be alive. The Russians were on the list, but out of his reach for the moment. Top of his list were the two scumbags that had used his beautiful Mimi, then casually beheaded her and cast her aside like a broken doll.

Tracking down randyjim6552 and tomcock85 had been easier than he had thought. Money spent on a computer consultant had soon narrowed the location. They had been tracked by the servers and IP address by their communications with Mimi via the swinger's site. A few more euros and helpful contacts in the French police yielded their whereabouts. He could virtually see them from his balcony in Monte Carlo. They were aboard the Lady Heloise.

Yerik's yacht moored in the marina.

He wanted them all dead. He wanted to taste and feel their deaths up close. He needed to know that he had consigned them personally to hell. The idea of putting out a contract had occurred to him, but he knew that no one in their right mind would go against the three Russians. Only someone with a death wish and nothing to lose, or live for, would contemplate such a contract, He knew that he was the ideal candidate for the job. He had little life left and he had nothing left to lose.

Benedict's physical strength was failing as the cancer ate away at him and in a short time, he knew, he would be incapable of taking revenge. He had to act now. There was urgency and desperation in his actions and it was that urgency that had led him to the Bel Air area of Marseilles. This was the drug capital of France. The area was a virtual no go area for the police, controlled by the drug dealers. It was run down and poverty stricken. Unemployment was rife and the inhabitants, mostly Muslim, were devoid of hope, opportunity and were without a promise of a better future, like himself.

There had been riots and the army had been used in the past when the police could no longer manage the area. Now it was virtually autonomous. Watchers observed all coming and goings into and from the area and phoned the information ahead to the gangs than run the estate.. Checkpoints had been set up to control entry and levies imposed on items brought in. There was a parking tax, but unlike the municipal scheme, where you were fined for non-compliance, here your car would be torched if you failed to pay.

Benedict knew that he was at risk as he soon became aware of the eyes on him as he entered gangland. His driver was Arabic and helped him make the contacts he needed in order to make the purchase he wanted. He though, was very nervous as he approached the first unofficial checkpoint. The cheap AK47s were openly on display as they pulled up.

The chauffeur spoke. There was a mobile call and they passed. This was repeated a further two times before they arrived at a low-rise block of flats. "I shall wait here."

Benedict alighted from the car and stood on the pavement waiting. He did not wait long. A young man of probable Turkish origin carrying a rifle appeared from the doorway and walked up to him. His French accent was worse than Benedict's, "follow me."

The hallway and stairs were mired in graffiti and the smell of stale urine pervaded the atmosphere. Discarded tin foil and needles were kicked causally to the sides of the stairs by the feet that entered day and night, on the quest for their owner's next fix. Benedict struggled to keep up with the youth leading him and was breathless by the time they approached the door to the apartment.

Words were exchanged and the heavy steel reinforced door was opened by another youth with a hand gun. It was clear that the contents of the apartment were valuable and were strongly defended. Given the checkpoints, the watchers and the armed guards it would be no mean feat to steal drugs from this gang.

Drugs were, however, merely a side-line for this crew, a means to finance and further their Cause. They passed through the passage way and entered a large cluttered room. The youth gestured for Benedict to sit on an old wooden chair off to the left side. He waited as a discussion took place between three men in Arabic. The room was cluttered with boxes and packets. Clearly a distribution hub for the various illegal activities the group partook in. The room was dominated by a covering, hanging from the long wall behind the men. The black and white Arabic scripted familiar banner of the Islamic State. Here, in this Muslim controlled area of Marseilles, they were operating openly with impunity.

The discussion over, two of the men departed taking their packages for delivery with them. The third man dressed conventionally and with no beard approached him as he sat waiting. "Mr Benedict," he said in an appalling French accent, which was even worse than the youth, he had first encountered. Benedict rose and responded in English. It was clear that the man had an English accent to his French.

He gestured for Benedict to approach a table in the corner where two chairs had been placed. "Please sit, do you have the money?"

In reply Benedict reached into his jacket pocket and placed the envelope on the desk between them. The contents were checked and he was offered tea, which he declined, only wanting to complete the transaction and depart as quickly as possible.

"I am intrigued as to why a distinguished gentleman like you would require such an unusual purchase?"

"I am not here to satisfy your curiosity, but you can rest assured, I am not involved in a religious crusade, but in an enterprise of a far more personal nature. May I have it please?"

"Of course," he got up from the chair and left for the next-door room, returning in less than a moment. He placed a large cardboard box on the table. "As ordered," he said

Benedict stood up and pulled open the lid to the box which had just been folded closed. He reached in and removed the vest and placed it on the table. It weighed less than he imagined.

"Are you familiar with how it works? Shall I demonstrate?"

Benedict indicated that he was unfamiliar with its operation and was instructed to remove his jacket. He was helped into the vest and stood uncomfortable in front of his instructor.

"This arms it. You complete the connection by screwing down. The light will come-on when you have done it. This pipe goes down your sleeve and you hold the bulb in your hand. Squeeze and hold. You detonate the device by releasing the pressure. If you are killed, the relaxation of your hand will trigger it. If it is not detonated, say by a freak that the hand is unable to freely move, say by you falling on it, the device will detonate if anyone tries to remove it. Is that clear?"

Benedict returned to the waiting car and the box was placed in the boot of the car by the AK47 welding youth. As he was driven back to Monaco, he was satisfied that he had enough high explosive to blow randyjim6552 and tomcock85, the Lady Heloise and the fucking Russians to hell.

Chapter 30

Harriet Shaw knocked on the deputy Directors door, she was eager to share her findings with Tim. "It paid off. "

Tim had been concentrating on reworking the staff schedules to cover the absentees that were away sick. Even MI5 was not immune from the influenza virus that was doing the rounds this winter. It took a brief second to refocus his mind.

"The passports?" she said.

"Got you, what do you have?"

"A British passport, that doesn't fit the profile. I obtained the details of all flights and passports for the dates and for men twenty to fifty years of age. I got nothing suspicious and started doing background checks, life style, jobs and education, cross matching for authenticity. Were they real people with real lives being lived?"

"And you found one that did not?" he was excited.

"No it was taking forever getting responses from all over the place. So I just had a look at the passport numbers, more as an exercise. I did maths and engineering and I thought I would, while waiting, for amusement, see if the passport number could be determined from the date and place of issue."

"Fascinating I am sure, but does it get us anywhere? I am sure there is a system to get the next number or something which they have sorted out for themselves."

"More than that it gives you the bio details, age, name, the date of birth and so on. That was not the number I was interested in. When a new passport is issued, or renewed it receives a new number. Passports are issued at various locations in the UK, by post and around the World. These numbers are like a phone book you can look them up. Can you see where I am going with this?"

"Not really?" Tim was not of a mathematical leaning

"I sat and thought about the details you gave me. If a new identity had been created for your killer, it would have to have been done very quickly. The other alternative is that he or she just used their own passport. So working on the idea that it was a rush and the recipient was British I did the obvious."

"I am not sure what the obvious is?"

"Look at the sequence, date and place of issue of the passports, in the target range."

Tim was becoming a bit irritated by the build up. "Look I don't want to dampen your enthusiasm, but is this going anywhere?" Harriett looked a little crestfallen. "Go on," he said.

She took a breath and continued in full verbal flight. "You can tell where a passport is issued and the number is of course unique to that passport. That is obvious, or you could have two people with the same number and the checks would be useless. First, I looked for fakes by checking all UK passports for duplicates. There were none. Then I looked at the actual issuing of the numbers themselves and posed a question. If you or I or someone doing a bit of spying, needed a passport in a hurry how would you get one?"

"That I can answer," said Tim. "The home office sends one over in a few hours."

"I figured that much myself," she was less than impressed. "But they are genuine passports and any details you want are put on them. No records are kept at the passport office for obvious reasons. Any junior employee could check out the details and pass on the information to an alien power. There have been numerous breaches in the past and they last thing the Security Agencies want is a list of spies and their passport details being sold on the internet."

"You need to help me here. You checked what passport numbers are not there on record?" said Tim.

"Exactly, I didn't look at the numbers that were there, but at the numbers that were out of sequence. Working backwards, if a passport was issued today at the UK passport office the number should be in a certain range, So using the bio encoded information on all the passports used and extracting the date of issue and place of issue I wrote an algorithm to estimate and compare the number that it should carry. One came up."

"Who?"

"Steven Melville."

"Show me," he said.

"There's the problem. The passport was not issued by the Passport Office, just a genuine number. There is no record, no application, no photo, but the passport is genuine. We have no idea what is on it, just a name on a passenger list. He flew into Crete the day after you did, flew back a day later and disappeared. I have a name and that is all but it tells us nothing."

"It tells us everything. It tells me that someone at MI6, or here, either provided a passport to the assassin who travelled to Crete and killed my wife. Someone is covering for the Russians. Now it gets difficult because there are numerous possibilities. Firstly the British Government, via possibly MI6, wanted the documents conveniently suppressed."

"Why would they want that?" Harriett asked genuinely shocked

"You are being naïve. The ex-Prime Minister, Tony Blair, did a good job of putting a stop to the investigations into British Arms export to the Saudis in the so called National Interest. There are billions involved on the trade with British Firms. There are plenty of reasons to cover up the fact that Russian black money may be being used fund the process."

"Who else would want to cover it up?"

"It could be a favour to the Yanks. Putin is running rings around them at the moment in Syria. They have no answer, no threat to employ and he is defiant in Syria and the Ukraine. The last thing they need is publicity that their sanctions, that are the only answer they have, are being completely circumnavigated. They are losing diplomatic face daily. This would make them look even more ineffectual."

"Is there anybody interested in outing the bad guys?"

"I am" said Tim, "And I shall find the murdering bastard and whoever is covering for him."

Chapter 31

Lifestyle resumed, the Driver was enjoying it to the full in the clubs of London. He was aware though that he still owed his old mentor twenty five million. He was tempted to not repay him, but he remembered what Benedict had told him when he had started out with him in the arms trade. "Leave enough in it for the next guy. You never know when you may want to do business with him again."

He picked up the phone and dialled. "Hambros? It is Jimmy."

There was a long pause. Benedict was surprised to hear from him. He toyed with the idea of just putting the phone down. After all, the man on the phone had been responsible for Mimi's brutal murder. He forced himself to listen, even though he just wanted the bastard dead," Hello."

The Driver recognised the awkward delay in the response, He was not surprised. If you owed someone twenty five million dollars and then ignored them, it would be only natural for them to be a little miffed." Look I am sorry for avoiding you. The deal went badly wrong. I lost the shipment and the Russians wanted their money. I just had to keep a low profile until it got sorted. How's Mimi?"

"How's fucking Mimi? She's dead you cunt," Benedict wanted to scream down the phone. He realised that the Driver had no idea that she had been killed or that he was to blame. He calmed himself and forced his voice to remain neutral.

"She's fine. Tell me what happened, I was a bit worried when you failed to answer my calls?"

"I got the launchers into Syria then the next thing I know the fucking Russian planes appeared and blew the lot to kingdom come, just before the ISIS bastards had paid me. I was fucked. I was left owing you twenty five million and the Russians one hundred and seventy five million."

"I am surprised you are still alive," wishing he wasn't.

"It was touch and go so I went to ground and then I had a stroke of luck. I got my hands on something the Russian bastards wanted."

Benedict did not care what he had or how he had acquired it. He was hoping that if he kept calm and showed interest, he would learn where the Driver was and somehow find a way to kill him." What do you have on them?"

"Just a stupid file showing what a bunch of scumbags they are. If the CIA had it, it would really shaft them. So they let me off the debt and gave me fifty mill to keep shtum. So I can pay you back."

The money was no use to Benedict now, he had weeks to live, but he feigned pleasure at the news. "I knew you would come good, but tell me about it." The more the Driver could be put at ease the more chance he had of locating him and killing him.

"It just fell into my lap. I got a tip off that this file was with dudes that were doing a trade with Yerik. I got on a plane to Crete and took it from them."

"Crete, why Crete?"

"Yerik had his big fucking boat parked there. He was swapping some tart for the papers."

"How did you get the papers then?"

"Messy, I just shot the Dude and the woman and took them."

"Fuck, you killed them? When did you become a murderer?"

"I had no choice, it was them or me. If did not get the file I was dead meat. I had no fucking choice, you see that? You would have done the same."

Benedict now was completely certain he wanted him dead. "Where are you?"

"In London, how do we sort out the money you are owed?"

I thought we might meet and I could hear the full story. We could settle up face to face, reminisce about the old times that sort of thing?"

There was a pause. The Driver was wary. He knew he had messed Benedict about and was one hundred per cent sure he was not happy with that. "Listen, I have a few loose ends to take care of. Give me a few days and I will sort it out. Got to go and I am looking forward to seeing you."

The phone went dead. Benedict checked the number on his handset, it was a mobile. He was worried that the Driver had suspected all was not well, but he had a least a means of contacting him and possibly tracking him down. It would have to do for now. He had other fish to fry today.

Monaco was quiet, there was an international poker tournament taking place at the casino but no other big events in town. The drive to the Marina was easy with none of the usual tourist traffic. His chauffeur dropped him a few hundred yards from the Lady Heloise and he made his way on foot to the quayside where she was berthed.

Sitting at the café under the tabac sign that overhung the pavement, he ordered his coffee. He had become a regular here, coming daily to watch the Yacht. He was impatient to take revenge, but he knew that the two killers where not on board. He would wait for their return. He would keep his vigil at the dockside for Mimi.

His regret was that there was so little time left. As he sat watching, he wondered how he could make Jimmy, the Driver pay. He had taken him from the streets in the States. He had given him work. He had made him a partner. He had passed on the business to him. In return he had caused the death of his wife. Not in person, like those two sadistic, callous murderers that had enjoyed abusing and killing her, but nevertheless he had caused it.

His doctor had called at his apartment that morning to discuss his end of life plan. "What a fucking joke, an end of life plan." He had a plan. A very simple plan, kill a load of fuckers and take them to hell with him.

He laughed to himself," so many cunts to kill and so little time."

Chapter 32

Tim was beginning to lose the will to live with the new MI5 awareness of cyber crime. It had become a hot topic of discussion in parliament, so they were liaising with everyman and his dog from GCHQ to more government advisors than he could shake a stick at. It was becoming hysterical with every expert identifying yet another area of weakness that could spell Armageddon for the Country. If all were to be taken seriously then nothing was safe. Social payments and benefits could be attacked. The mail could all be misdirected with an attack on the automatic postcode sorting system. The car taxation and registration was vunerable with millions potentially lost in revenue and unregistered cars driving everywhere.

He was in the middle of writing another brief for the Home Secretary on the latest set of fears when Harriet knocked on his door.

"Come in," the door opened and before she could cross halfway he asked. "What do you know about a likely cyber attack on animal passporting with specific reference to sheep?"

She looked blank. "Call yourself a computer expert?" he said.

"Are you serious?"

"Semi, it is an issue, we can't have sub-standard meat entering the food chain. It is one of a list of fears raised by the advisors to the various ministries. Since the Russian attack on the US automated Presidential polling system every Minister wants to look like they are on top of cyber related activity in their area of responsibly."

"I see that. We don't want a cell of sheep spying for the Russians do we? God knows what the security implications are with rogue sheep roaming freely around the country."

"Exactly, get on to special branch and make sure they are on top of the undercover shepherd training programme." He laughed, "What have you got for me?"

"Just more of the same, Hambros Benedict and his wife's murder, the police reports are very detailed and graphic and it is pretty well established that it was not just a run of the mill murder. The timing is of interest to us as well. Her death ties in perfectly to this Jimmy Riddle, Steven Melville, whoever he is and the Russians and the Baltic Bank."

"Do you have a theory?"

"I sort of do, but it has lots of holes filled in by guess work. Look, we know that Benedict is trying to get out of the arms business. We know that if he is not in the arms business then, whoever this Riddle is, now calls the shots. We know the Baltic Bank finances a deal for him to buy arms. We know something goes wrong and he can't pay them back, or at least they for some reason write off the debt and even give him more money. All this at the time that the same Russians have taken your wife to trade for the file you have on their operations. The file is stolen and the debt goes away."

"You think that Benedict's wife is murdered because they want to send out a warning that they mean business and want their money back. Then they decide they don't want their money back and write the debt off because?" he paused.

"Because this Riddle, Melville character had got his hands on something more valuable, that they will accept, in payment."

Tim's gut was telling him that Harriet had worked it out. Whoever this Jimmy Riddle was, he had travelled to Crete on a fake passport issued by some branch of the Security Service, killed his wife and stolen the file. Then to save his own neck, he had traded it to the Russian scumbags in exchange for his debts to be written off.

"The problem is that we have no idea who this Riddle is and are no closer to finding out," she said

"We have one lead, Hambros Benedict. He knows him better than anyone."

She walked round his desk pulling a chair with her, "May I"

She sat at his terminal and started pulling up files," All we have on Benedict."

There was lots of information over his arms dealing career. At one point MI6 had used him to gather information for them. He had dealt with every major rebel and drug lord in Latin America at some point, selling all of them guns. He had been a good source of background information which MI6 no doubt shared with the CIA.

"He may be an arm dealing scumbag but he seems to be a patriotic arms dealing scumbag, willing to help where he can," observed Tim.

"Where does this get you though?"

"It gets me to the point where I think I need to ask him who this bloke is."

"What, are you just going to go up to Benedict and say, by the way I am from MI5 and would you kindly tell me all about you and your partners illegal arms dealing activities? You think that will work. Do you?"

"Do you have a better plan?"

"No"

"Then it will have to work. I want the bastard who killed Jeff and

Dealer

my wife."

Chapter 33

The last time Tim had walked the streets of Monaco it had been the day of the Grand Prix. The rain had been falling all morning and it was still drizzling at the start. The street had been crowded with people and every bit of available space had been occupied by stalls selling memorabilia and souvenirs Now the streets were quiet as he made his way to the Marina.

This is where it had all began. The Lady Heloise was still moored in the harbour, quiet now, not crowded with party goers. He could not help but remember with sadness the friendship he had with the Turkish translator and part time intelligence officer, Yosuf. He recalled their journey together and desperate struggle to stay alive. Yosuf had lost that struggle, killed by his ex-boss, Turkish Intelligence operative, Mehmet.

It could hardly believe it was just a few short months ago. He had met, fallen in love and married the most wonderful woman in that short time. The deaths just kept mounting as did his loss, his wife, Yosuf and his best friend Stiles, all gone. It all seemed so futile. So much suffering and pain for the greed of just a few men.

He made his way along the quayside and saw the diminutive figure sitting outside the café. Benedict had his coat pulled up against the inclement weather. The summer was over and the wind was beginning to blow, the water in the harbour rising and falling with the gusts causing the million dollar yachts to bob up and down. There was the sound of clanking as chains and ropes relaxed and tensed with the movement of the boats.

As Tim approached the figure, it was clear that this man was not the same man as the photos portrayed on his file. He had shrunk and his pallor was a grey. The grey Tim had seen in the face of his mother as her last days approached. The cancer was spreading rapidly and Benedict's body was breaking down as the fight was being lost to its unstoppable progress.

He sat at the old man's table. "You are watching?"

Benedict ignored him. He was fearful at the stranger's arrival and even more fearful at his opening statement.

Tim continued, "You are watching and waiting."

He was forced to respond, "I don't want to be rude, but I do not wish to talk."

"You are watching the Lady Heloise are you not?"

Fear now entered into Benedict's mind, he feared that Tim was one of the Russians thugs sent to settle matters. "Who are you?"

"I am a man looking for someone. I am not here to hurt you."

Benedict looked at his table companion as coffee was delivered. He did not know this man, but he knew intrinsically that he was not one of the goons that accompanied Yerik to the Lady Heloise. That did not mean however that he wished to engage with him. "Please respect my wishes."

"I cannot," said Tim, "it is too important to me. I need you to answer some questions.

"Who are you?"

"My name is Anthony Burr, I work for MI5."

"I do not deal arms anymore. I am retired. I really have no interest in it any more. I have nothing to say."

Benedict turned his face away and gazed in the direction of the Lady Heloise. Tim had not been sure what to expect but was not surprised that this man had turned inwards. His wife brutally murdered and facing imminent death by cancer, it was hardly surprising that he had no interest in Tim's problems. Tim knew though that this man was his only link to the mysterious traveller to Crete, Riddle or Melville, the only suspect he had in the murder of his wife. Only Benedict would know who this man was and could expose his identity to Tim. Time was running out and this might be the only opportunity Tim might have to speak to him before the cancer claimed him.

Tim pushed on, "I am looking for a man, the man who was your partner. He goes by the name of Jimmy Riddle or Steven Melville?"

There was no reaction from Benedict who continued to look towards the yacht, waiting for the return of Mimi's killers. He had no interest in helping MI5. He hated Jimmy, the Driver, but whilst he had caused his wife's death, he had not cut her head from her body and the deaths of randyjim6552 and tomcock85 were top of his list. Whoever this Tim was, he was only interested in the Driver, not for some government inquiry or some such thing. The one thing MI5 was not, was an assassination squad. The one thing Benedict wanted for the Driver was his untimely death. The man sitting at his table certainly did not look the part of a merciless killer, he looked more like a pen pushing civil servant.

Tim realised he was not connecting with Benedict and was beginning to fear that he would never get the information and that his wife's killer would never be punished. He had to try and engage him and spoke again.

"I have been on the Lady Heloise, it is owned by a scumbag called Sokolov Yerik. He likes to hurt people"

"I know this."

"You want him dead?"

There was no response from Benedict. Yes, he wanted him dead and he wanted him in hell. He wanted Jimmy, the Driver, dead and he wanted him in hell. He wanted randyjim6552 and tomcock85 dead and he wanted them in hell. With luck, he would take some of them to hell with him. He would not let this MI5 man divert him. He would not risk missing his chance to kill these bastards personally. He would not risk Anthony Burr interfering in his last chance at vengeance. He ignored him.

Tim sat there and starred in the middle distance. Harriet had been right, this was no plan at all. There was no reason for this man to help him. His journey had been fruitless. He felt frustrated as he saw his chance of ever avenging his wife slip away. The realisation that his life was only fuelled by a desire for revenge shook him. He remembered another man who had spared his life called Mem or Annubis, a hired killer. Like His life had been driven by the need for revenge. In the end anything he might have been had been eroded, just being a killing machine that neither lived nor loved.

He looked at Benedict and tried to think of something, of anything that might get him to open up about Riddle. "It is personal," he said.

Benedict turned for the first time and looked at Tim. He studied him slowly before turning back to his vigil of the Lady Heloise. He saw in Tim another desperate man who was looking for retribution. He was not persuaded however to divert his own cause to help this man. They shared hatred and that was all. He believed Tim when he said it was personal, but he needed to take this final path alone, no distractions.

Tim left ten euros on the table and pulling his coat around him he stood up. He was desperate and felt that the chance of finding Jackie's killer was fading into the distance. He wanted to scream at Benedict, plead with him or threaten him, but he knew the dying man before him was treading his own lonely path and would not be distracted.

"I am sorry about your wife. My wife was murdered in Crete a few weeks ago, so I do know how it feels. I am truly sad for both of us," Tim said as he started to leave the café.

The word Crete burned in Benedict's brain. Jimmy had boasted of Crete. Was this the man whose wife the bastard had murdered? It was clear to him now, this man, this MI5 agent, this Tim was sent to him to wreak vengeance on the Driver. It was destined to be. Here before him stood the means of his retribution. This man would kill Jimmy for him. He would not just have the death of the bastards who had killed Mimi, he would have the death of the man who had been the cause of her death. Tim would be his avenging angel.

"Come to dinner tonight."

Tim stopped and was about to ask what had changed his mind, but decided that might break the tie.

"The address is..." began Benedict.

"I know the address," interrupted Tim

"Of course you would," said Benedict, before resuming his watch of the Lady Heloise.

Chapter 34

Tim and Benedict stood on the terrace overlooking the Start Finish straight of the Grand Prix circuit. The wind had stopped with the coming of nightfall and the sea was tranquil in the moonlight. In contrast to the mood of the two men, all was peace and tranquillity in Monaco.

They had stood in silence holding their drinks. Tim was reluctant to push for answers and Benedict was still assessing the man from MI5. Neither wanted to pre-empt the situation and frighten the other off. They both had murder in their hearts, but their brain ordered caution.

"Tell me about your wife," said Tim.

"What shall I tell you? I was a lot older and she was an ex-prostitute. Of course, foolishness and money was branded about. I saw it differently, I bought many things in my life, and none lasted long. Shoes, suits and jewellery all have their moments, but even if you buy a work of art, you can never keep it. You die and title is relinquished. So why not buy a woman that gives you pleasure and company in your old age?"

"What about love? "

"Are you a romantic Mr Bur?"

"Call me Tim, please. I didn't think, it was a jaded outlook from my first sortie into marriage I suppose. Then I met Jackie only six months ago and it was an instant connection. So in answer I am a convert to romanticism."

"Love is fulfilling, but now I find hate more sustaining. Mimi freed me. She had no inhibitions. She was pure in that sense, like a primeval being, like an animal. It worked in its way and in my way I loved her greatly. They took her from me in the most cruel and vile manner."

"The Russians?"

"Yes, the Russians. Not for any reason, not as a punishment, just a message to be sent. She was no more than a letter to Jimmy. Pay up or you are next."

The dinner was on the table. Benedict's chauffeur was now the cook and the butler and signalled they should sit. They moved in and sat at the table. Benedict poured wine and they were left in peace to serve themselves.

"Tell me of your Jackie"

"There is so little to tell. It was so brief. I sometimes wake in the mornings and wonder if it really happened. In months we met, feel in love, married and she was murdered. Ultimately because of the same scum that killed Mimi. We share that at least, love hate and loss."

The mood was sombre and they ate for a while in silence, each locked in their own memories. The atmosphere was interrupted when the next course arrived.

"What makes you think that my Jimmy murdered your wife?"

"I cannot be sure. I am hoping that you might fill in the blanks. If I tell you what I have learned and figured out. Will you do that?"

"I am not sure Tim. I have so much conflict in my mind. I am facing my own mortality, loss of my wife and it seems betrayed by the closest person in my life. I just don't know. Tell me and I will think and see how I feel."

Tim relayed the saga of the file sent to their home and Jackie's abduction by Yerik to trade for its recovery. He described how he had returned from shopping, to their apartment in a hotel in Crete and finding the file gone and his wife and Stiles murdered.

"What brought you to my door?"

"The money, I followed the loans from the bank owned by the Russians and it led to you and more specifically to your partner Jimmy. I have also tracked the movements of a single male going under the name of Steven Melville who came to Crete and left, coinciding with the murders. The file goes missing and then the Russians no longer seem to be bothered by the money lent to your Jimmy. I think your partner, this Melville and the murderer are the same. I am hoping for two things from you, one, the identity of this Jimmy Riddle and two, that you can confirm my theory."

"What will you do to Jimmy if he is the killer of your wife?"

"Kill him," Tim said with icy simplicity.

I should like for you to do that, do you promise me that you will carry it out. I want him dead, not in prison, dead and in hell with me. Do you solemnly promise Mr Burr that is the course you will pursue?"

"I do. I want the bastard dead. I want it so badly I can taste the vengeance on my tongue."

"Very well, Jimmy came to me to help buy weapons to sell to ISIS in Syria. He was financing it with his own cash and a loan from the Russians via the Baltic Bank, but he was short, twenty five million short to be precise. I lent him the money. Bear in mind we had worked together for nearly fifteen years one way and another. Then instead of paying the money back he disappears and I cannot contact him. The next thing that happens is that the Russians turn up at my doorstep looking for him and kill my wife to send a message." Benedict stopped talking and his grief was pitiful to watch.

Tim said nothing while Benedict recovered his focus." Something had clearly gone wrong and Jimmy must have lost the shipment and failed to get the payment. A few days ago, I get a phone call from him out of the blue saying that all is fine and he is paying me back. He clearly did not know that things were far from fucking fine and Mimi was dead."

Tim said, "Did he say anything else, anything that ties him to the death of my wife?"

"The cunt killed your wife and friend. He said he had been to Crete. You have your murderer Tim. Now kill the fucker for my Mimi and your Jackie."

Tim was stunned, he did not dare breath. He had his answer, but only a name, no face, no identity. He needed more from Hambros Benedict. "I can't identify him. You have to tell me all you know."

"I don't know his real name. I have always known him as James Riddle. In this business people try not to want publicity."

"Do you have a photograph of him?"

"No, he was careful. He called himself the Driver because he used to race. You may be able to track him that way."

"Is there anything at all that could lead me to him?"

"He must have some sort of connection to the UK Government or a powerful friend. He could always seem to conjure up a passport anywhere he was if he was in trouble."

"Anyone can buy a fake passport if you have the money," Tim said.

"Not fake, they were genuine UK passports. Once in Colombia he was being hunted by the Government and he went to the Consulate and he just picked up new travel documents in a different name."

There was no doubt that the Driver had murdered his wife, Benedict had confirmed he had links to one of the security agencies, backing up what Harriet had deduced from the passport numbers. He was no closer to identifying the Driver, he felt despair creeping into his mind.

"I have one thing, his mobile number," said Benedict.

Tim's pulse rocketed, "Got the fucker."

Chapter 35

"Well, how did it go?" Tim was sat at his desk in Thames House and Harriet had taken the seat opposite. He had arrived back from his meeting with Benedict, no further advanced in his quest to find the location and identity of the mysterious Driver, He did know that he had the killer of his wife and the motive.

"I have a phone number, so I want you to trace the owner."

"At last something I can do easily," she smiled. "Do you want to tell me what I am looking for? All I have been looking for are transaction relating to the Baltic Bank and associates. I am curious what you learned from your visit to Monaco."

"I don't think that is a good idea. Can you tell me who the phone is registered to?" She was tapping her tablet as he spoke.

"Just a minute," she continued to input the details. He sat in silence and felt his anxiety levels rise. Was this the moment he would learn who killed his wife and friend Stiles? He felt his heart racing as he tried to maintain his calm.

"Not registered, I am afraid," he felt the disappointment. He had the urge to actually cry with frustration.

He forced himself to think. "Can you access the phones records?"

"Of course, but the phone company will need a warrant to release them."

"I could authorise it under the counter terrorism laws."

"You could, but you would need an oversight signature, Elaine Wilkins could countersign the authorization?"

Tim found himself in a dilemma. The head of MI5 had warned him off twice in his pursuit of the Baltic Bank. Could he realistically go to her and ask her to instigate a breach of privacy on a matter that was clearly nothing to do with MI5? She would more likely pass the matter to the police or MI6. This was personal. He wanted this bastard to himself and he would not trust it to the police or others to prosecute. He had already tried and passed sentence on the Driver. That sentence was death.

"Is there any other way of finding the owner? He asked

"I could track it, or at least get the phone company to send us a history of it location. See which radio masts it pings. Where it stops at night should give you roughly where the target sleeps."

"Won't you need a warrant?"

"No, I'll just add it to the watch list. One more won't be noticed. What with the police, MI6, Immigration, Special Branch, us and God knows who else tracking phones, the phone company routinely does it. Trust me, no one will take a second look."

"Do it, please?"

She left and he made a phone call. He then went in search of Stiles and his luggage that had accompanied them to Crete in their mission to rescue Jackie. He soon ascertained that the Diplomatic box, with their flake jackets and guns, was still on the premises. He left his office and made his way to the storage area in the basement.

There was an air of the scholarly to the storage area. Miss Pembury approached him as he entered. She was part of the fixtures and fitting of Thames House. The Service, of course, now had all its material digitalised and ready at the push of a button, but she still kept "useful stuff" as she called it. Most of the papers had been moved to a storage facility, but somehow she had retained most of the interesting historical artefacts. Her pride and joy were notes from Winston Churchill, written at the height of the Second World, often completed late at night after imbibing. They were a National Treasure.

"Do you still have the box I took to Crete?"

"I do. I haven't got round to emptying it or returning the bits and bobs. It's the paperwork. If I leave it long enough someone usually turns up looking for the stuff. I say, send me a copy of the paperwork and hey presto it is all done for me."

"Good plan, can I have a look?"

She walked him through room after room, mostly full of old boxes and accumulated paraphernalia that had built up over the years." I couldn't interest you in a few World War gas masks could I? All the rage you know." She pointed to a pile of boxes in one corner. Eventually she located the box.

He lifted the lid and began to rummage. "You won't take anything without signing for it?"

"I am the Deputy Head Ms Pembury, you can trust me to follow procedure," he smiled.

"Let me know when you are done," she wondered off leaving him to it. He soon located the gun and ammunition. Checking she was not looking he shoved the gun in his belt at the back and headed for the exit.

"Did you find what you wanted?" she called distractedly, as he left.

When he returned to his office Harriet was waiting for him, "you have the phone details?"

She pushed the phone's locations across to him. "The pattern is irregular but, in general, this seems to be where the user often spends the night." She pointed to the GPS coordinates she had written on the first sheet of paper.

"Bring it up on a map?"

She tapped on her tablet and the street view came up. It was semi-rural. He scrolled around. There were not many houses compared to an inner-city location. "Thank you, I'll take it from here."

Now it would be elbow grease and luck. He began his search of the voting register and land registry. It was slow, he began to develop a headache as he looked intently at the results, fearful that he would miss something. It dragged into hours. He began to fear that he had missed something and would have to go through the data again, trying vehicle registrations or traffic prosecutions.

Then it just hit him. One name stood out. It was a name he knew. He had the Driver, now he would have revenge for his wife. He left Thames House, taking the gun and knowing he was about to become a killer.

Chapter 36

All good things come to he who waits and Hambros Benedict had waited and it had paid off. He walked slowly along the Monaco quayside, it was truly a slow and painful process. He wanted to savour the experience ahead of him and had not taken the pain relieving cocktail of drugs that morning.

The colours of the World seemed to be more vibrant and alive this day. The blue of the sky was bluer. The yellow of the sun was bright and intense. The air was clearer and fresher. His life experience was magnified despite the pain he felt in his failing body. He was alive at this moment in time, as he faced his final moments on this Planet.

Benedict paused to rest. His progress was slow, hampered by his lack of strength. As he caught his breath, he looked up towards the heavens. A golden shaft of sunlight shone through the white wispy clouds and illuminated the water in the harbours, a flash of gold in the green and blue. He looked at the clouds and in their formation, he clearly saw his Mimi, arms outstretched, reaching down to him, beckoning for him to join her. He caught his breath and with renewed energy, continued his journey to the Lady Heloise.

He had watched yesterday as the fleet of cars arrived at the yacht, The Bentley and the two Mercedes had driven to the quay. He watched as Yerik stepped from his car and he waited to see who was among the entourage in the two Mercedes. He was rewarded, as from the cars randyjim6552 and tomcock85, his wife's murderers, stepped into his view. They all boarded the boat.

For a brief moment he panicked, fearing that the Lady Heloise would put to sea, but she remained and was still moored as he walked along the jetty.

He felt destiny was on his side, that the gods favoured him. Little things had convinced him that he was about to take his revenge. The entrance to the quayside had no security to stop anyone walking along, boarding the million dollar yachts and just helping themselves to the contents. Some maintained a resident crew while the owners were absent. Others were devoid of human activity in the winter.

The garbage was collected regularly, maintenance workers came and went on a daily basis, He had merely walked up to the gates some hour earlier and had been assisted through by a kind hearted maintenance worker, his tailored clothes being sufficient to convince all that he was the sort of man who had a boat in the marina.

Things further played into his hands in the security of the Lady Heloise herself. He had noted that the crew all sat down to eat lunch at around one o'clock each day, leaving one member to guard the deck. He would, however, take the opportunity to sneak off and meet with his girlfriend. She was crew on another vessel, moored further along the quay, so the Lady Heloise was unguarded for the lunch period.

He finally finished his slow walk along the jetty, making sure to remain hidden from view, he looked at his watch. Soon the deck would be deserted and he could board. Time seemed to pause as he waited. His heart rate increased with the mix of fear and elation he was feeling. He took deep breaths and fought the pain that was steadily increasing in his cancer riddled body. He tried to focus elsewhere and push the pain to the back of his mind. He thought of Mimi and the terrible end she had been subjected to by the murderous, unfeeling bastards who were on the boat just metres from him. He thought of his conversation with Tim. He was saddened that he would never know if the cause of his grief, Jimmy, would receive the death sentence promised to him by the man from MI5. The wave of pain subsided and was replaced by determination as he watched the deckhand disappear for his lunchtime rendezvous with his girlfriend.

Hambros Benedict stepped forward and walked slowly up the gangway. He stood on deck for a moment getting his bearings and listening. He could hear the chatter of the crew faintly talking over lunch and nothing else. He was mindful that he couldn't just wander around blindly looking for his two murderers. He had to make a choice, up or down. He went down the steps to the stateroom.

Fate again intervened and he was rewarded by the sight of one of his wife's assassins entering the panelled door into the room. A second earlier and he would have walked into him face to face. A second later and he would have missed seeing his back as he entered the room.

He pushed the door and entered. He was rewarded to see randyjim6552 and tomcock85 and the rest of Yerik's goons gathered together, helping themselves to a buffet lunch laid out on in the centre of the opulent and ornate room. He was disappointed that Yerik was not in the room, but felt in his heart that all aboard the yacht would soon be dead.

The speed of reaction by the goons surprised Benedict. He had barely stepped through the door before he was challenged.

"Who, the fuck are you?" said tomcock85.

It was clear that the ravages of his cancer had caused Benedict's appearance to change dramatically. His skin, like ageing parchment, was stretched over his emaciated frame. His eyes were recessed deep in their sockets and his parlour was the grey of death. "Don't you know me?"

Gun now in hand, tomcock85 peered more closely at him, as he stood calmly in the doorway. Benedict's fear and uncertainty had passed, his pain was gone with the elation at confronting the scum who had taken his beautiful Mimi from him.

"I do know you," he turned to randyjim6552, "it's the sad cunt whose wife we fucked to death."

"What are you going to do Granddad? Throw your false teeth at us?" he mocked.

"I am going to kill you."

"No you aren't," laughed randyjim6552 and fired his gun. The bullet hit Benedict cleanly between the eyes and he fell to the floor, spun onto his right side by the force of the impact, trapping his right hand underneath his body.

"Don't let him bleed on the fucking floor, the boss will go mental," they joked as tomcock85 approached the body.

He looked down at the old man laying at his feet and spat. He hooked his foot under the body and rolled it over to ensure that he was dead. It was the last thing he did on this earth.

As the body was rolled, Benedict's grip was released on the bulb connected to the suicide vest. The blast was spectacular. The band of security men were vaporised instantly. The whole top of the Lady Heloise was blown to a million pieces and the blast spread gas and flame throughout the whole vessel. The shock wave was so intense it caused the boat to jump from the water. The explosion was so loud it could be heard two miles away. The plume of smoke could be seen for five. As the effects of the blast radiated out from the yacht, glass was shattered in the buildings and boats in the immediate vicinity.

Then calm and silence, deadly silence. The beam of sunlight shone down on the burning wreck, as if putting it in a golden spotlight and Mimi's cloud arms seemed to reach down from the sky and reclaim his soul.

The bomb was later identified as of ISIS manufacture and the Jihadis, not ones to miss out on publicity, claimed responsibility for the bombing. It was added to their tally of atrocities on the Cote D'Azure that year.

Chapter 37

Tim sat at his dining room table, around him he had gathered together the things that he held dear. Morning broke and the Sun was just rising, as he opened his Wedding album. It sent shafts of light streaming through the gap in the curtains drawn across the French windows.

He had not been able to bring himself to look at it before. He slowly turned the pages. The wounds were still raw in his heart, but the memory of their Day was already beginning to fade. Almost with new eyes, he viewed their brief life together. There was Jackie, leaving her Dad's house with Daniel, her son. He looked at the small boy dressed in his wedding suit, posing and smiling. He had developed a real love and affection for the little chap and it was reciprocated then. Tim had vowed to bring her back to him safe and well.

He had failed, Daniel's love and respect had turned to loathing and hate. When he told him that his Mum had died, the little boy had lost his World. His words now rang in Tim's head once again. "I hate you. You promised. You killed my Mummy." He now refused to see Tim and lived with his Grandparents.

Tim turned the page, there was a picture of Jackie steping into the wedding car. She was so beautiful in her wedding gown. She smiled the tender smile he loved. Her hand was posed on the open door and he could clearly see the engagement ring they had chosen together on her finger. He recalled the moment she had said "I will," and he had placed the wedding ring on it.

He smiled through the tears as he recalled their Honeymoon on the Nile. The tiny shower he could hardly fit into on the boat, the chaotic hot air balloon ride and crashing in a cane field. He felt her body close to him and the comfort of her kisses. Now gone, taken from him by the Driver.

Another page another photograph, there were his two ushers, Stiles and he lined up in their top hats and tails as though dancing. They all had big smiles and were doing jazz hands. He looked closely at Jeff Stile's face. He needed to remember him like that. He wanted rid of the final image that burned in his mind. Jeff slumped in that chair on the terrace in Crete, a hole in his forehead and cats lapping his blood.

There was Jackie's Mum and Dad standing proudly by their daughter. They had not been immune from the Russian's search for their paperwork. The home invasion and attempted abduction of Daniel had left her mum with limited use of her arm where she had been shot and her father would never recover his speech fully, or his mobility after his stroke. Such a high price had been paid by all of them for a few men's greed.

There were the group photographs. He could make out Elaine Wilkins, his boss, and her son Nick in the background among the sea of familiar faces, distant relatives and old friends of them both. He closed the album and holding back the tears pushed it away from him.

The old child's book, in Arabic, tired and tatty with use over the years drew his attention. He allowed it to fall open to where its previous owner had viewed it the most often. The owner was the assassin who had twice entered his life, called Annubis. Tim knew little of him, but knew that he treasured this book, given to him as a child, presumably by someone he loved.

The book opened naturally at the scene of the passing of the soul into the afterlife. Thoth, the ibis headed god, stood to the left recording the proceedings as scribe. The balance scales were in the middle, a feather on one side and the soul of the departed on the other. Annubis, the Jackal headed god, presided over the weighing while Sobek, the crocodile god, waited to take the souls found heavier than the feather to the underworld. Isis waited to escort the souls without sin to their place in the heavens, to become stars.

Tim closed the book and knew that he had weighed and passed judgement on the Driver, that judgment was damnation. Tim would feed his sole to Sobek and ensure his passage to hell.

Chapter 38

Tim had to contend with the queues on the M25 at the Queen Elizabeth II Bridge before he turned off at the Bluewater shopping centre and headed for the village of South Darenth. He had located the Driver's house easily, being by far the largest property in the Kent Village. Located on the corner of two roads, it occupied nearly three acres. He drove past the Drive on Roman Villa road and saw the double gates leading to the swimming pool complex ahead and the stables further down. He turned right at the end of the road and parked a discrete distance from the property.

He walked back up the Holmesdale Hill and found the side entrance. It was a small gate with a post box to one side. He entered and climbed some steps past the now, leafless rose bushes. He found himself at the rear of the property looking at the grass tennis court. He was conscious of his heart beating as he passed the rear windows. He saw the kitchen at the end of the property that backed on to a paved courtyard. This was his hope of gaining access without being seen.

He tried the kitchen door and found it unlocked. He entered cautiously and drew the gun from his overcoat pocket. He passed through the utility room and found himself in a large farmhouse kitchen on his left and a huge dining room off to his right that could be seen through double glass doors. He crossed and slowly opened the internal door.

To his right was the front door and steps going up. There was a reception room directly in front of him with etched glass doors and to his left was an open door to the rear reception room. He could hear the sound of shooting and explosions emanating from it.

The door being ajar, he made his way quietly in the direction of the sound of the gaming console. He pushed the door further open so he could gain a better view. He felt his hand tense on the gun as he sidled into the room.

He need not have been concerned. The Driver was sat with his back to him, totally immersed in his Play Station. He stood behind him and pointed the gun at the back of his head. He thought of just pulling the trigger and blowing his brains across the room, but he remembered that Stiles and his wife had the last view of the killer face to face, as he callously put a bullet into their faces.

He walked to the front of the Drivers chair and stood in his view. He was so engrossed in his game that he did not notice Tim standing there with the gun aimed at his head. Gradually the presence of someone in the room dawned on him. He started and dropped the joy pad, his mouth hung open. The noise of the game continued as the Driver sat frozen, fear across his face and wide eyed.

"Hello Nick, time to pay your dues," said Tim.

Nick Wilkins, the son of Elaine, head of MI5 was stareing unbelieving at Tim. He was paralysed, stareing at the gun. "How..." he struggled to speak.

"How did I find you? Hambros Benedict gave me your phone number after the Russians, you owed money to, murdered his wife." Tim's voice was emotionless as he readied himself to fire.

"Don't kill me, I had no choice. I only meant to steal the file to get the bastards off my back. I just walked straight into Jeff and your wife. I had no choice, they both knew me from your wedding."

"So you just blew their brains over the terrace and took the file to save your arse. " Tim levelled the gun at Nick's face.

"I wouldn't do that." He heard Elaine's voice behind him. She had been in the house and entered the room behind him. He looked and saw that she had a gun pointed at his head.

"You can fuck yourself. You are as guilty as he is. He came to you didn't he when his arms deal fucked up and the Russians were after him. It was you that hid him in an MI5 safe house. You weren't happy in just keeping him alive. Were you?"

She said nothing and kept the gun trained on Tim's head.

"Then you saw your chance to save your precious, worthless piece of crap of a son. You had me and the file in custody in Thames House. You let me and Stiles keep the file and go to Crete with it to save my wife. It was out of character. You would have played it by the book and handed the file to MI6. It was so out of character that I should have known earlier, but I ignored it. Your saw your chance to save your precious son. You knew that Yerik, Lesta and Nikhil would do anything to have that file. You helped me out of your own self-interest. You protected Stiles, Jackie and me from the Russians for one reason only, to send your son to take possession of the file whatever the cost. Jackie and Stile's lives counted for nothing as long as Nicholas was safe?"

"He is my son. He is my only son. What else could I do?"

"You could have prevented the murder of my wife you fucking bitch. Oh, you helped me get her back. You organised it all for Stiles and me, the guns, the bullet proof vests, the diplomatic passports, the Special Forces and even the Navy. You did everything you could and broke every rule, just to make sure that we kept the file. If the trade had taken place the Russians would have had their incriminating evidence back and Nick would have lost his only chance to stay alive."

"I didn't mean for your wife and Stiles to die. I am sorry" Elaine's face was contorted, with remorse. She was in a state of emotional turmoil. She had worked her all life to ensure the security of her

Country. She had desperately tried to keep her son on the right path. Time and time again he had been in trouble, she had pulled strings. She had called in favours and even helped him with fake passports and documents to enable him to escape justice. Whatever he did, he expected his Mother to come and save him. From a small boy it seemed he had been missing some vital part of his personality. She had spoiled him and he had never had to face the consequences of his actions. His Mother was there to be used to get what he wanted. He had no sense of right or wrong. He just did and took what he wanted and was outraged, if his Mother did not do his bidding.

"You provided him with a passport, an MI5 passport in the name of Steven Melville, which is why I couldn't trace it. You arranged our accommodation and told Nick where we were staying. You then made sure that the Special Forces who rescued us gave the file back to us rather than hand it to naval intelligence. It was imperative that we retained the evidence on the Russians, as that was Nick's only chance of saving his worthless skin. That is what happened wasn't it? You set us up from the very start?"

The sound of the shot shattered the silence. Tim felt no pain, dazed by the loudness of the retort.

Nick's face briefly turned to surprise in the instant before life left him.

Tim looked at Elaine, the gun still in her hand. She mouthed her last silent words as tears ran down her face "I am sorry," she put the gun to her head and pulled the trigger.

Tim stood for a moment. Then he returned his gun to his pocket. It was the third time in his life he had held a gun and people had died, but he had never fired a single shot. He turned and left. He felt no emotion, no satisfaction. The souls weighed, Annubis and Sobek satisfied, justice had been served.

Chapter 39

Harriet Shaw sat opposite Tim in the office. Thames House was in a state of lock down. Elaine's death had shocked and terrified in equal proportions. No one was sure what was happening. Tim had taken control, insisted on calm and maintaining order and discipline.

"I don't understand it," said Harriet.

Tim sat in silence observing her for a few moments. She became aware of his gaze and felt uncomfortable as he continued to stare at her. Finally he spoke. "I think you do," he finally spoke.

"How could I?"

"I have been thinking and now matters are clearer, he let the sentence hang.

The silence, now awkward forced her to speak," What matters?"

Tim swivelled his chair so he faced the window to his right, turning his gaze from Harriet. He could feel the tension in the room. He let her sweat a little longer.

"You betrayed me..."

She started to protest but he ignored her and raised his hand to bring silence into the room once again. He slowly started speaking. Choosing his words, he carefully laid before her the sequence of events as he now understood them.

"You were new, fresh faced and a techie. I had no experience of cyber space or its security implication. In fact, I was the least qualified person on the Planet to take on the role at MI5 to expand our counter intelligence in that area. But I was chosen to head up the recruitment drive. "Why do you think that was?"

"I don't know?" she said reluctantly.

"I think you do. In any event, Elaine placed me in the driving seat. New to the job and with no specialist skills in computing it puzzled me at the time. Of course, I did not care, as the only reason I stayed at MI5 was to use the resources to track down Jackie's killer. The day to day stuff was just an irrelevancy."

He looked at her to see if she reacted to the revelation. She now had taken on the role of looking out of the windows, avoiding his gaze. She turned her head and bowed her head avoiding eye contact.

"I needed help, technical help. There you were. You really did help, but you did so much more. Didn't you?"

"I don't know what..."

He again held his hand. "Elaine had to give me the job. There was no viable alternative at that point. There was disarray and Government pressure. I was close to the situation and answers were needed. I would be dedicated to getting those answers. In fact, I would be more than dedicated, I would be fanatical, after all, it was personal. The last thing Elaine wanted was the truth. The fact that she had conspired and was involved in the deaths of her Deputy and an employee's wife was not something to be broadcast. "

Tim watched Harriet's reaction. There was none. She knew. She was smart and had worked it out.

"I was out of my depth and Elaine approached you, "What did she offer, rapid promotion, more pay?"

"Nothing really, I think she made me feel important I suppose. She painted you as a potential rogue agent. I was naïve and she used that."

"So she put you in my eye line and I took the bait. I used your skills to track the money, the passports. You knew every step of my investigations and you told her?"

"I thought I was doing the right thing."

"Who knows? I suspect that at some stage she would have asked you to hinder the investigation in some way, if it got too close. withhold something or change something."

"The passport, but I didn't. I was becoming aware something was badly wrong. In any event, once Benedict confirmed the details of the murder, I realised the truth would come out."

"Did you know her son Nicholas was the assassin?"

"Of course not, I wouldn't have become involved, if I had known..."

"But you worked it out, when?"

"I had shown Elaine, your search of the properties that were local to the phone mast that pinged, on Nicholas's mobile number, given to you by Benedict. She didn't look at the map or anything. It was clear that she already knew. I came back here, looked at the properties and like you I identified the safe house connection. It fell into place. She had from the start been only interested in protecting the murderer. It was only a small jump to work out the only person that could be."

Tim looked across at her. "What do you think now?"

"I am not sure. I am sorry. It was a mistake. What are you going to do?"

"What I do best, nothing," said Tim. "You go back to work and we shall let the gods decide what happens next."

She left and Tim pulled the tattered book from his drawer. He opened it to the page showing the Weighing. "It is not finished yet. I will have my revenge," he vowed.

Nicholas E Watkins

Oligarch

Also by Nicholas E Watkins

Tanker

Dealer

Bank

Steel

Hack

About the Author

Nicholas Watkins lives on the Coast with his wife and has four children

He is a retired Accountant and has a Degree in Economics. He worked in the City of London for many years.

Dealer

Copyright © Nicholas E Watkins 2017

The right of Nicholas E Watkins to be identified as the Author of the Work has been asserted by him in accordance with the Copyright, Designs and patent Act 1988.

All rights reserved. No part of this publication my be reproduced, stored in a retrieval system, or transmitted, in any form or by any means without the prior written permission of the publisher, nor may be otherwise circulated in any form of binding or cover other than that in which it is published and without a similar condition being imposed on the subsequent purchaser.

All characters in this publication are fictional and any resemblance to real persons living or dead is purely coincidental.

Nicholas E Watkins

Chapter 1

Aleena heard the news that her husband had been killed in the fighting in Mosul, Iraq, not with a sense of grief, but with fear. She was fourteen years of age and had travelled with her sister and her friend to Iraq, just four months ago. They had been seduced by the ISIS propaganda on the internet, with heads filled with dreams of playing their part in the restoration of the Caliphate and a perfect World in which they fitted, they had left Walsall and headed for Iraq. They were to be brides to the brave fighters in a Holy War.

Their dreams soon evaporated like early morning mist, as the reality of the situation was revealed. Her sister and friend, Mariam and Haniya, had become the camp whores. They had no choice. The Jihadis used any unmarried women that way. To justify their actions, they would brand young girls as unclean. Unclean could mean anything from using tampons, to shaving their pubic hair. Anything would do in order to justify the mass raping of young women in the local population, or so called Jihadi brides from abroad. It made no difference. All in the name of Allah and always justified by some obscure and misinterpreted verse in the Qur'an

She had been more fortunate in that she had not been raped to death in the preceding months. She had been taken by an ISIS lieutenant as his bride. Her being more fortunate was relative. He was old with rotting teeth, rotting body and a rotting soul. He had used her as he wished, enjoying the privilege he had to take and keep a young girl for himself to the full. She had never felt so much pain as he had inflicted on her young body. She now constantly bled from her anus, which was completely prolapsed, from his brutal attention.

She was glad he was dead, but she knew that she would be just another whore in the camp, to be gang raped by all the heroes of the Jihad. She huddled in fear as night approached. She had crawled through an opening in the wall to one of the partially collapsed buildings in the compound. She could hear the sounds of shelling in the distance, as she burrowed into the loose rubble in an attempt to conceal herself.

ISIS was losing ground on all fronts. In Syria, Assad's forces, supported by the Russian air force, were driving them out. In Iraq, they were being driven from the territory they held by the Iraqis and the Kurdish forces and the battle for Mosul was almost lost. Morale was low and discipline was breaking down. The fanaticism remained, but was insufficient on its own to win a war.

"Where are you, British slut?" she could hear them getting closer, looking for their evenings entertainment. They called, mocking as you would call your dog. "Here whore, come slut, come, fucky-fucky time."

She tried to hide in the dust and filth of the rubble. She closed her eyes, as if that would have the effect of making her invisible. As if, not seeing the beam of their torches searching the bomb site of what had been a village, would make them not see her. "There you are bitch." Roughly, she was dragged from the building into the compound, where the camp fire burned.

Three women were already being used by the group of, thirty something odd, men. "Another whore to fuck boys," shouted her captures, as she was dragged into the light. Her clothing was ripped from her as she was thrust into the centre to join the gang rape in progress.

She was pushed face down into the dirt, her bottom exposed to the group of men leering at her young, not fully formed body. "Look at her arse hole," said one.

"Fuck me, what a fucking mess. That's been well fisted and fucked."

"Looks fucking nice to me" said another, as he shoved her face further into the dirt and shoved his hard penis, fully in. She screamed in pain as he pushed her prolapsed anus back into her body. The pain was terrible as he thrust with no form of lubrication.

"Fuck, that feels good," he cried as he ejaculated. The queue formed as they waited their turns.

Nizar had had a shit day. He was supposed to be in command. The idea of command was rapidly descending into the theoretical. The Iraqi troops were squeezing them in the South and the Peshmerga were linking up in a pincer move so, the ISIS forces would soon be split in two, The Peshmerga were the troops of the autonomous Kurdish region of Iraq. He knew they were lost. The allies, led by the US, the Russians and local Syrian and Iraqi forces, would regain the ground ISIS had held up until now. It was only a matter of time.

He sat in the Jeep, on his own, looking at the flashes of light over Mosul. The bombardment was incessant now. He had enough of this fucking shit. He had been fighting for four years non-stop. He was losing faith in the dream. It had seemed so different, in what was a lifetime ago, at University in Leeds. Then, he had believed. The lure of a pure Islamic state had seemed so beguiling. In England, he had been disgusted by the society with its secularism and its corrupting influence on his brothers and sister. A land run, in accordance with Sharia law, was what his fellow students and he, who attended the Mosque, wanted. Not the corrupt secularism, in which they lived.

Dealer

Now he was older and battle weary. The atrocities he had witnessed by ISIS on fellow Muslims, in the name of Allah, had started the worm of doubt burrowing in his mind. He had doubted his faith, which was once so all pervading. He had begun to doubt his own humanity. He was the leader in this sector and he had participated in the beheadings, the rape and the torture. It was all so black and white, when he had begun. If you didn't agree with the ISIS doctrine, you were an enemy and that justified everything.

Nizar no longer believed and he wanted to go home. He started the engine and drove towards the compound.

Aleena was screaming and praying for death as yet another Jihadi began to bugger her. She did not hear Nizar's jeep drive into the compound. The raping soldiers of ISIS paid little heed either as their leader drove up. He stepped from the jeep and looked at the scene with disgust. So this was what he was fighting for. This was the dream he had seen in his minds eye in the Mosque, listening to the Imam's preaching in England. The reality, he now knew, was a crock of shit.

He looked at the girl being gang raped, no more than fifteen or sixteen. Something snapped. He had come to issue the orders and outline this unit's plan of action for the next day. Now, he just wanted them to fuck off.

He snapped. He unleashed a burst of gunfire into the night sky. He had their attention. "Stop fucking and listen to me." They formed a circle around him. He gave the usual bullshit, morale-boosting talk and outlined their role in the next days fight.

They listened, but were eager to return to their evening's entertainment. Their time was running out. They would fight and continue to fight, but they would soon die. The force against them was now overwhelming and it was only a matter of time. There might be virgins in paradise awaiting them, but there was pussy closer to hand now.

He finished his speech, then said, "I'll take the girl."

They were reluctant, but defying their commander was not an option. She gathered her clothes and made her way to the jeep. "Get in."

She sat like a bundle of rags in the back, as he drove away from the compound. She looked at him fearful, expecting them to stop at any moment. What was his particular perversion that made him reluctant to use her in front of the crowd?

"We're going home," he said to her surprise, as they drove west.

Chapter 2

It was early December and the morning was cold, wet and grey. The press were gathered outside East Finchley Crematorium. They sensed there was a bigger story out there, but they just couldn't sniff it out. A Mother and her son were to be cremated today. A Mother who had shot her own son and then had turned the gun on herself was a big story. But, when that Mother had also been the Head of MI5, then it was a truly big story.

They knew there had to be more. They wanted to know what was going on at MI5. Only two months previously, the Deputy Head had been shot in Crete along with the wife of the now acting head, Anthony Burr. They knew that something was going badly wrong in the Service, but they could not ferret out the details.

The inquest into the death of Nicholas Wilkins, at the hands of his Mother Elaine, ruled unlawful killing. No motive was established and vague evidence was introduced, questioning her mental state. Although it made no sense, that the head of MI5 seemed to have left her office, drove to her son's house and shot him. That was what had, apparently, happened. There was no evidence of any third party involvement. She shot him and shot herself. Questions were asked in the House, but not answered. National security was paramount and revealing details of Elaine Wilkins's current operational involvements would not be in the best interest of the Country. That was the line and it was being held to.

The death of Jeff Stiles, the then Deputy Head of MI5 and Jackie

Burr, the wife of the now acting head, Anthony, was just as obscure. There were many unanswered questions, surrounding their murders, but few answers. Mr and Mrs Burr had finished they honeymoon and had meet up with their colleague in Crete, before returning to the UK. Both had been shot, execution style, but the Greek police had made no progress in tracking down the killer.

The one man, who knew all the answers, was Anthony Burr, now head, at least for the moment, of MI5, but he had no intention of filling in the blanks. He was known as Tim. It was a schoolboy nickname that he had found hard to shake off.

Tim Burr stepped from his MI5 issue Jaguar XF and followed, by the driver, who had previously served Elaine, walked passed the press to the Crematorium. The building was modern and red brick. Owing to the drizzle, many of the mourners were gathered under the portico, which afforded some shelter from the drizzle. Tim stood alone, waiting for the hearse to arrive.

This last year had been the stuff of nightmares. He had nearly been killed by terrorists and hunted by the Turkish Secret Service. He had met and married a beautiful woman, had her snatched from him and murdered with his best friend Jeff Stiles. He had found his wife's killer and seen justice done. Her killer had pulled the trigger, but Tim knew that the reason that bullet had been fired, was that men more powerful than the killer, greedy men, had set in motion a chain of events that led, ultimately, to her slaying.

Tim had unfinished business with these men. They had not ordered his wife's murder, nor had they pulled the trigger, but their ambition, greed and thirst for power, had led to the murder. They were her true assassins. For now, they were untouchable, but Tim knew his time would come. Now, as acting head of MI5, he had the resources to hurt these men. He determined that he would bend all to their destruction and they would pay. No matter how long it took, or where they went, he would exact retribution.

Both the Foreign Secretary and the Home Secretary were among the mourners. They arrived separately. Tim knew them both and they acknowledged him. The head of MI6 appeared. All had their security in tow. As more great and good arrived, the number of Special Branch officers assigned to personal protection began to swell, until they formed a small security army. Not only were the Special Branch represented en-mass at the funeral, but the police were highly visible around the Crematorium and spread throughout the local area. There was a massive MI5 undercover presence in Tim's honour, but also to protect the thirty, or so, of his staff from Thames House, who had known and worked for Elaine.

The Prime Minister could not attend. Her duties overseas had prevented her, but the Foreign secretary, Terrance Mailer, who had been with her, had flown back to attend. Tim and Mailer had history. Mailer had been indiscrete in the past and Tim held the evidence that could see him and prison and wreck his life. Tim had used this evidence before to his advantage and he knew that he would again in the future. Tim held Mailer in contempt and knew that he should, rightly, be imprisoned, but that did not matter for now. That could wait. For now, he would do what he had to do to settle the score with the men who had been responsible for his wife's death.

He understood that he was a compromise as head of MI5. He had neither the experience, nor the expertise, for the job. What he had, was the fact that he was alive. He also, had the support of Mailer, purely for his own self-preservation. Tim, however, was good at the job, even if his underlying driving force was revenge. In fact, that revenge gave him an intensity that the service had been lacking under Elaine Wilkins.

The hearse arrived, driving slowly up the sweeping drive, past the garden of remembrance to the side of the building. Elaine's cremation was not the first, nor would it be the last of the day and the flowers in the garden bore witness to that fact. The arrival of the hearse, signalled to the mourners of the previous ceremony, that it was time for their departure.

They followed the coffin in. Elaine's husband followed the pallbearers, pushed in his wheel chair by his brother. Tim followed the two senior Government Ministers, who in the turn followed her immediate family. Her son, Nicholas, was already laid to rest at her local Church. So they were spared the double service. The fact that Elaine's husband had only a few days ago buried his son was apparent in his whole demeanour. He was bewildered and uncomprehending of the tragedy that had occurred. He had not expected to outlive them, but fate had left him alone, to bury his wife and his only son. He had been told that he had only weeks to live five months ago. Fate had been unkind to him, by allowing him to survive long enough to put him through this.

The service was simple and the eulogy was delivered by the priest. Her husband, even if he had wished to say something, could no longer speak clearly, as the paralysis crept incessantly onward through his body.

The curtain opened and the coffin rolled from view to the waiting flames. They trooped out through the side entrance and gathered awkwardly, in silence, into the garden of remembrance. The rain was falling harder as they stood waiting for a respectful interval to pass so they could make their departure without unseemly haste. There was to be a gathering after, but for the Government Officials to attend, they would have filled the venue with so many security personnel as to make it impractical and turn it into a circus. In any event, the presence of so many reporters was already disruptive and no one wanted to add to the situation.

Tim was about to leave when Elaine's husband beckoned to him. He made his way over to the frail man seated in the wheelchair. Tim shook his hand and offered his sympathies. He struggled to understand his speech. His condition had worsened to such an extent that even talking was a challenge. Tim looked to her husband's brother, for clarification.

"Come to the house."

"I shall certainly try, I will find some time and organise it." Tim had no real desire to visit and was making the appropriate response expected of people in these circumstances.

Tim saw this as an opportune moment to restate his commiserations and depart. The man in the wheelchair however, became agitated at Tim's obvious lip service to convention.

His bother took Tim's arm firmly." He insists that you come to the house. It is important apparently. He says Elaine had something there."

"What is it? "

Tim struggled to understand what her husband said in reply. He looked to the man's brother for clarification. "He does not know. He has allowed no one to touch it. It is marked secret."

He looked down at the dying man in the wheel chair and spoke. "I shall come tomorrow. Again I am so sorry for your loss."

Chapter 3

Rafiq wandered down Afghanistan Street to the Three Idiots Restaurant. The rumours were running thick and fast through the Camp. It was inevitable that the Calais and French authorities would have to act to clear the migrant camp, known as the Jungle. Its population was getting close to the ten thousand mark now and was almost a small town with shops, restaurants, nightclubs and even hairdressers. The inhabitants had congregated on this patch of land on the French coast with the common goal of, somehow, getting across the Channel and into the UK.

The Jungle was to be cleared and the French Police, with bulldozers, were assembling. Busses had been arranged to distribute the refugees throughout France and register them. Many, in the Camp, had had enough of living in tents, shipping containers and roughly constructed huts made from scrap. They were leaving for the busses and would start their new lives in France. Others were not so accepting and would not give up their efforts to get cross the Channel. It was this group that Rafiq was interested in.

Sitting in the plastic chair outside the restaurant eating his meal of chicken and rice, he observed the hustle and bustle of camp life. There were plans to start fires and destroy the camp before the Authorities took full control.

"What is happening my man?" Rafiq called to a fellow Afghan, who approached the restaurant.

The young man joined him, with his meal costing about three

euros. "We are not going quietly. We intend to torch the camp tonight. Are you with us?"

With a full mouth, he nodded. Rafiq knew it was important to stay at the centre of things. Hidden among the genuine migrants, he knew were groups whose purpose was not to seek asylum, but to wreck terror and death on the UK. The summer onslaught on the European Borders, by thousands of refugees fleeing the conflicts, across the Middle East had given these terrorist an unprecedented opportunity to get their people into Europe.

"Some of us are planning to move further along the coast and start a new camp."

"Count me in," said Rafiq.

Rafiq, had over the last three months, made sure his credentials, as a man with extreme views, had been spread around the inhabitants of the Jungle. His hard line views had made many wary of him and they made a point of avoiding any association with him. Others had been drawn to his fundamentalist beliefs. They were the people that he and MI5 were interested in.

He was part of the recruitment drive, undertaken by the Secret Service, to ensure they could effectively monitor the Islamic community in the UK. Prior to 9/11. MI5 had historically been focussed on home-grown terrorists such as the Irish. They had been ill equipped to deal with the threat from the Middle Eastern groups. Predominantly white and with no links to the Muslims in the Country, they were disadvantaged in their counter intelligence role. It had to change.

Efforts were made with varying degrees of success. Rafiq, not his real name, was part of the drive, to recruit agents who would blend into the Asian and Muslim community. Following the terrorist attacks in France, in which some of the perpetrators had gained access to the Country posing as refugees. It became imperative that the Jungle needed to be infiltrated. MI5 had taken the lead, as it was considered a counter espionage operation, rather than MI6, who themselves were playing catch-up with Russia, now again added to its list of potential enemies. Along with China, the Middle East and North Korea, MI6 were running to stand still.

Rafiq found himself moved from a comfy flat share in Leicester, to a wet muddy tent outside Calais. Life as an MI5 agent was far less glamorous than he thought it would be when he applied for the job after leaving University. He had been born in the UK. His parents had been in the UK when the Taliban took control in their homeland. They had just not bothered to go back and were granted asylum. They had started a small business and had been reasonably successful. His Mother had not really bothered to learn English and he had consequently grown up bilingual. Only having conversed with his Mother, he developed her regional accent and local vagaries of speech, which made him sound genuinely Afghani.

Over the past months, he had been successful in identifying potential suspects and passed details back to Thames House, the headquarters of MI5 in London. These details had been shared with France and the other EU Countries so their activities could be monitored. The French and others, of course, had their agents circulating in the Jungle as well and he had popped up on their lists as a potential threat. Their agents, had in turn, been added to his list. The various countries secret services would, eventually, sort it between them.

He had spotted the young couple a week ago. They stood out to him. They seemed like genuine refugees at first glance. Rafiq had made it his business to get on the impromptu welcome and orientation committee for new arrivals. This gave him a good opportunity to vet the new arrivals first hand.

The man was in his late twenties and the girl was younger, under eighteen he guessed. They were posing as man and wife. Rafiq felt that there was something amiss. He had developed a feel for the normal inhabitants. These stood out. Firstly, the majority of the arrivals were young men on their own, or in groups. A young couple was far rarer. There was also something about the male that grabbed Rafiq's attention, something about his demeanour that set him apart. It took awhile for him to put his finger on it, but eventually, it became clear in his mind. He was a battle-hardened soldier, not a traumatised civilian fleeing Syria, Iraq or other area of conflict. Something set him apart, confidence, the way he moved, Rafiq was not sure of the indicator, but something set off the alarm in his head.

He made a point of getting close to the couple. Immediately the man spoke, he had his confirmation. The accent gave it away. He was British. The girl also gave their origin away when she spoke, which she tried to avoid doing as much as possible. Rafiq was pretty sure she was a Brummy, or had lived somewhere close to Birmingham.

He knew that the two were, most likely, returning terrorists trying to get back to the UK and avoid being arrested. He was right; Nizar and Aleena had made their way back from Mosul and wanted to get home. They were stuck in Calais however.

That night, fire began to ravage the tents and huts in the Jungle. They had to leave. They couldn't join the queues for the busses that would settle them in France. They could not risk registration. Any inquiry would expose Nizar as a high placed officer in ISIS. As the flames and smoke rose into the night sky, over the camp, he and Aleena gathered together the meagre possessions and made to leave.

They headed north along the coast, avoiding the French Police ringing the camp, under the cover of darkness and the confusion wrecked by the inferno, now raging. Nizar had no plan, but knew the Jungle now afforded no protection for them. Aleena clung to him, still fearful and totally dependant on him. He pulled her close. She had suffered so much and he had given so much for something that neither of them now believed in.

Rafiq followed them as they walked off into the cold and lonely night.

Also by Nicholas E Watkins

Tanker

Dealer

Bank

Steel

Hack